BILLY SURE

· KID ENTREPRENEUR ·

INVENTED BY LUKE SHARPE
DRAWINGS BY GRAHAM ROSS

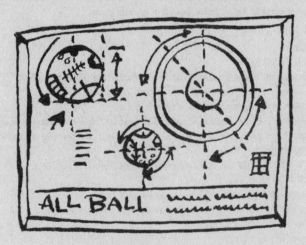

ALL BALL

Simon Spotlight

New York   London   Toronto   Sydney   New Delhi

SIMON SPOTLIGHT

An imprint of Simon & Schuster Children's Publishing Division
1230 Avenue of the Americas, New York, New York 10020
First Simon Spotlight paperback edition May 2015
Copyright © 2015 by Simon & Schuster, Inc. Text by David Lewman. Illustrations by
Graham Ross. All rights reserved, including the right of reproduction in whole or in
part in any form.
SIMON SPOTLIGHT and colophon are registered trademarks of
Simon & Schuster, Inc.
For information about special discounts for bulk purchases,
please contact Simon & Schuster Special Sales at 1-866-506-1949 or
business@simonandschuster.com.
Designed by Jay Colvin
The text of this book was set in Minya Nouvelle.
Manufactured in the United States of America 0415 OFF
10 9 8 7 6 5 4 3 2 1
ISBN 978-1-4814-3948-0 (hc)
ISBN 978-1-4814-3947-3 (pbk)
ISBN 978-1-4814-3949-7 (eBook)
Library of Congress Catalog Number 2014949478

Chapter One

Backstage at Better Than Sleeping!

I'M BILLY SURE. YOU'VE PROBABLY HEARD OF ME. Wait, that sounds weird, like "Who is this kid and why does he think I've heard of him?" But it's not like that. I mean, I'm not like that. And you probably weren't thinking that anyway because . . . well, like I said, you've probably heard of me. Because I'm *that* Billy Sure, the famous kid entrepreneur, inventor, and CEO of **SURE THINGS, INC.** At the moment I am also the kid who is sitting on a blue couch in a plain little room backstage at the **Better Than Sleeping!** show.

Maybe you will see me on the show tonight, if your parents let you stay up that late on a school night. (If not, maybe you can watch it in your room with the sound turned way down. Just don't get caught—I don't want to be the kid who gets your TV taken away!)

"You're bouncing your legs," Manny tells me. Manny Reyes is my best friend. He is also the chief financial officer of Sure Things, Inc., which is just a fancy way of saying he likes crunching numbers and has a really smart head for business.

I didn't even realize I was doing it. I look at my legs. Reason #35 why Manny is the greatest CFO: He is always right. My knees are definitely bouncing like Ping-Pong balls on a trampoline.

"Don't do that when you're onstage," Manny continues. "It makes you look nervous. Don't pick your nose, either. Or burp. Or throw up. Definitely don't throw up."

"But I *am* nervous. I might throw up," I say.

Manny gets a puzzled look on his face. "Why? You've been on TV before."

"Just the local news. This is national TV. Millions of people will be watching!"

Manny grins. "Exactly. This is a fantastic marketing opportunity. So don't blow it!"

"Way to make me less nervous," I reply, grabbing my knees in an attempt to stop my bouncing legs.

My dad leans forward. He's sitting at the other end of the blue couch. "You'll do great, Billy. We're proud of you. I just wish your mother could be here."

My mom travels a ton, as a scientist doing research for the government. I don't know much more than that. She's been on assignment for a while now, but she knows all about what's been going on with me because we e-mail a lot.

"Why do *I* have to be here?" my sister, Emily, moans. She hasn't looked up from her cell phone in three hours. "I'm bored, hungry, and thirsty."

"I couldn't just leave you at home while we

came to New York, Emily. That'd be illegal," replies my dad.

"I'm fourteen!" she argues, keeping her eyes on her phone. "And very mature for my age. I'm perfectly capable of taking care of myself!"

"Sure you are, Ninja Spider," I taunt her. Lately Emily wears only black. Black shirts, black pants, black shoes, black everything. That's why I've nicknamed her Ninja Spider.

Emily finally looks up from her phone to glare at me. She wipes her blond bangs out of her face. Everyone says we look alike, which is weird because she's a girl. She notices my legs are bouncing again, despite my best efforts to stop them.

"A kangaroo called. He wants his legs back," she says.

Before I can think of a comeback, a can of soda appears in front of Emily's face. "Soda?" someone asks. "I heard you say you were

THE SODA

thirsty. In the room across the hall there's a fridge full of free drinks. Stuff to eat, too. Chips. Candy. Fruit, if you're feeling healthy."

Emily, being in a classic Emily mood, takes in a deep breath. I know her well enough to know that when she exhales, she'll snap that she doesn't want a soda; she wants to go home. But before she speaks, she looks up and sees who is holding the can in front of her.

DUSTIN PEELER!

I'm sure you know who Dustin Peeler is too. (See? I don't just say that about myself. Not that I think I'm as famous as Dustin Peeler.) In case you don't know, Dustin Peeler is the most popular teen musician on the planet at the

moment. He can sing. He can dance. He can walk on his hands. He can play guitar, piano, drums, English horn, and didgeridoo—upside down. And according to Emily, he is the most gorgeous human being who ever graced the earth with his presence.

Dustin Peeler smiles his perfect smile, teeth glistening like ocean waves on a sunny day. Emily's mouth drops open, her jaw practically scraping the floor. "Thank you," she manages to squeak out as she takes the can of soda. Her knees begin to shake.

"No problem," he replies.

"Now who's part kangaroo?" I whisper, pointing discreetly to Emily's shaking knees.

But Emily ignores me. She still can't take her eyes off Dustin.

I try again. My sister is seriously making a fool of herself, and I feel like it's my duty to let her know. "Emily," I whisper a little louder this time. "You look really dumb with your mouth hanging open like that!"

And then Dustin Peeler notices me for the

first time. "Hey, you're the All Ball dude! That thing is awesome!"

"Thanks," I say.

An assistant sticks her head in. "Dustin, we're ready to do your hair."

"But his hair is already perfect," Emily says like she's in a trance.

"Oh, they're just doing their jobs," Dustin says, smiling another dazzling smile. "Have fun out there!" He gives us a double thumbs-up and leaves. Emily resumes breathing.

"Who was that?" Dad asks.

Emily sighs.

"He said the All Ball was awesome," Manny says. "Maybe we could get him to do an endorsement of some kind. Or even write us a jingle!" Quietly singing, "All Ball, All Ball . . . the only ball you'll ever need," Manny pulls out his phone and taps a note to himself.

I told you Manny has a great head for business. He has a ton of brilliant ideas about how to sell Sure Things, Inc.'s products. Without Manny, I wouldn't have a business, just a bedroom full of inventions. And dirty laundry. And a few hidden candy bars (okay, maybe dozens).

Emily pulls out her phone again and immediately starts texting all her friends that Dustin Peeler just handed her a can of soda. She even texts a picture of the can. "I'm keeping this can forever," she announces.

"Be sure to rinse it out," Dad says.

I guess it was cool to meet Dustin Peeler. I've never bought any of his songs, but I've certainly heard them. But I am much more excited about the other guest on **Better Than Sleeping!** tonight. Manny spots him first, standing out in the hallway.

"Hey," he says. "Isn't that the baseball player you like? Carl Somebody? The shortstop?"

"Like" is a slight understatement.

Carl Bourette has been my favorite athlete since I was in kindergarten. I have every Carl Bourette baseball card. Carl Bourette bobbleheads. A nearly life-size poster of Carl

Bourette, hanging on my door. I know all his stats. His favorite kind of bat. What he puts on his burgers.

My brain is screaming, "CARL BOURETTE!"

But my mouth is saying nothing. My jaw is hanging open, but no words are coming out. Possibly a little drool, but no words.

"Might want to lift your jaw off the floor, genius," Emily suggests.

Then Carl Bourette notices me staring at him. Instead of getting as far away as possible from the weird kid with the staring problem, he smiles and starts walking over to me.

"Hi," he says, shaking my hand. "I'm Carl Bourette."

"Billy Sure," I manage to murmur.

Carl nods. "That's what I thought. You invented the All Ball, right?"

Now it's my turn to nod. "Yes," I say. "I did." I seem to be limited to one-syllable words and two-word sentences.

"I agreed to do the show tonight because they told me you were going to be on it," he says, chuckling.

WHAT?!

"Man, that All Ball is great!" Carl continues enthusiastically. "My kids love it! Heck, my *teammates* love it! We've got one in the locker room!"

DOUBLE WHAT?!

I can practically see Manny's eyes turn into dollar signs. He whips out his phone and taps another note to himself.

"Thank you," I croak, keeping to my one-syllable, two-word rule for talking to Carl Bourette.

Carl reaches into his jacket pocket and pulls out a pen and notepad. "I'm sorry to do this, but would you mind signing an autograph for my kids? They'll be so excited I met you!"

Carl Bourette just asked *me* for *my* autograph?

What kind of bizarre, backward world am I living in? What next? Emily asking for my opinion on her outfit?

"Sure," I reply. "You got it." Three words in one sentence! A new record for talking to Carl Bourette!

I sign a shaky autograph on the notepad and hand it back to him. "Thanks!" he says. "I really appreciate it."

Before my head can explode, the assistant hurries back into the room. "Billy, we're ready to do your hair."

Carl laughs. "Bet you thought you knew how to do your own hair. Welcome to being famous!"

Chapter Two

Catch!

NOW I'M STANDING NEXT TO THE CURTAIN, WAITING to walk out onto the set of *Better Than Sleeping!*, where I will be interviewed by the host, Chris Fernell.

In my hands I am holding a carrying case. Make that "in my very sweaty hands." I'm really nervous. I can't help it.

Behind me another assistant places his hand on my shoulder. I have no idea why. All I know is that I'm supposed to enter when Chris Fernell says my name.

"Please give a warm welcome to Billy Sure,

kid entrepreneur!" I hear from onstage.

As the studio audience applauds, the assistant gives me a little shove to start me walking. Maybe some people get so nervous they freeze.

I walk out onto the set, remembering to smile. I don't know if you've ever been on a television set before, but it's *bright*. Also, the furniture seems smaller than it looks on TV. In fact, the whole set seems kind of small. And there are big cameras pointing right at me. *Now would be a really terrible time to trip,* I tell my feet.

Chris Fernell shakes my hand and motions for me to sit in the chair next to his desk. I have never understood why TV hosts need desks. Do they have homework they need to work on during the commercials?

"So you invented the All Ball, and now this

thing is huge!" Chris begins. "How old are you, Billy?"

"Twelve," I say. "Thirteen next March."

"Twelve years old!" Chris marvels. "When I was twelve, I was just playing video games. And not complicated video games. Simple games. You know, like, 'click on the door to open it.'"

The audience laughs. I don't think what he said was very funny, but it seems weird not to laugh, so I do. *You need to work on your fake laugh,* I tell my mouth. *That didn't sound very good.*

"When did you invent the All Ball, Billy?" Chris asks. He seems genuinely interested. Of course, that is his job.

I explain that I actually came up with the idea for the All Ball last year in sixth grade, but I had trouble figuring out exactly how to make it work. But then at the very beginning of the summer, the trouble all went away and it came together. (At least, that's what I tell him. The real story is much more complicated than that. But I won't be telling any of that to

14

Chris Fernell.) Instead I talk about how Manny started a company with me called Sure Things, Inc., and we found a manufacturing company to make the product.

"The product," Chris repeats, smiling. "I love that! You're twelve years old and you've got a product! Can we see it?"

The audience applauds again. I open my case. "Here it is," I say, bringing out two All Balls. "It comes in two sizes: large and small. Wanna play?"

The only ball you'll
ever need.

The audience whoops and cheers. They want to see Chris play. "Sure!" he says. "Let's do it!"

"Great. Let's start with soccer," I say. Then without anyone seeing, I press a button on a remote and the All Ball turns into a soccer ball.

We walk over to the side of the stage, toward the band, where two goals have been set up. I set the small ball aside and toss the larger All Ball to Chris. "How does it feel?"

"Like a perfectly normal soccer ball," he says. Then he drops it on the ground and kicks it toward me. I kick it back. Chris works the ball with his feet a little, but lets me steal the ball and kick it into the net. "GOAL!" Chris shouts. More applause.

"Okay, now what if you wanted to play volleyball?" I say.

"I love volleyball," Chris says. "But we need a different ball."

"No, we don't," I say, taking a small remote control out of my pocket. "That's the beauty of the All Ball."

I press a button on the remote. And the ball changes from a soccer ball to a volleyball. Just like that.

"That is amazing!" Chris yells. We hit the ball back and forth. "Incredible! It's exactly like a volleyball! How did you do that?"

"I'm afraid the ball-morphing technology is patented, proprietary, and top secret," I say, using all the terms that Manny has coached me on. I gesture toward the basketball hoop set up on the stage. "I see you've got a basketball hoop."

"Why, yes we do!" Chris says, hamming it up. "If *only* we had a basketball!"

I press a different button on the remote, and the volleyball in Chris's hands starts turning into a basketball. It grows. The seams move. The surface changes. And the ball turns orange.

The audience loves it. Chris dribbles the ball and shoots a layup, which he makes. The crowd *really* goes wild at that one.

"Okay," Chris says. "This All Ball is, like,

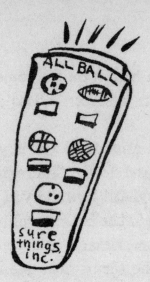

the most amazing thing I've ever seen. Soccer ball to volleyball to basketball, unbelievable. But I've got to ask, what if I want to play football? No way, right?"

"Actually, way," I say, pressing another button on the remote control unit. With a kind of **ZZZWOOP** sound, the basketball shapes itself into a football.

Chris stares at the football. "Okay, now you're freaking me out. How? Huh? *What?*"

As Chris tosses the football to the drummer in his band, I remember another one of the things Manny told me to say. "The large All Ball eliminates the need to buy and haul around five different balls. Now you just have to buy one."

The drummer tosses the football back to Chris. Tossing it from one hand to the other, he turns back to me. "Hold it," he says. "I'm no mathematician, but I'm pretty sure you've only shown us four balls—soccer ball, volleyball, basketball, and football. What's the fifth ball?"

I aim the remote control. I don't mean to time it this way, but I hit the button just as Chris tosses the football into the air, ready to catch it in his other hand. **Zzzwoop!** In midair, the large All Ball morphs from a football into a bowling ball. "Catch!" I call out.

Naturally, Chris isn't prepared to catch a sixteen-pound bowling ball, and drops it. **Clonk!** Luckily, the bowling ball doesn't land on his foot.

I let out a sigh of relief. I totally don't want to be that guy who goes on TV and injures the host. Chris looks up at me in surprise and then starts cracking up. The audience roars with

$1 + 1 + 1 + 1 = 5?$

laughter, and then breaks into a long round of applause.

It is cool. No, it is awesome. I look around and have trouble believing that this is really my life.

"Can I try one of those? Maybe the small one?" someone asks.

It's Carl Bourette! He appeared on the show earlier, but now he's walking back onstage! The audience starts cheering even louder!

"Hey, Billy," he calls. "Toss me that other All Ball!"

Carl Bourette remembered my name! He just said it out loud! On television!

I run back to my seat, grab the small All Ball, turn it into a baseball, and toss it to Carl. I'm no pitcher, but luckily it goes right to him. "Nice!" he says, tossing the ball up with one hand and catching it in the other.

"Get out your remote," he continues. "And zap it just as I toss this to Chris. Ready, Chris?"

"It's not going to change into another bowling ball, is it?" Chris asks, pretending to be nervous.

HERE IT COMES!

"Here it comes!" Carl says, throwing the ball at Chris.

I hit the remote. **ZwoinK!** The baseball turns into a hockey puck midair! Chris catches it and holds it up over his head in triumph.

"Looks like I'm missing all the fun," someone else says. The audience starts going nuts. I look to see Dustin Peeler strolling onto the stage.

So I, Chris Fernell, Carl Bourette, and Dustin Peeler play catch, changing the small All Ball from baseball to hockey puck to tennis ball to golf ball to Ping-Pong ball.

When Chris gets a signal that we are out of time, he puts his arm around me and shouts, "Billy Sure and the All Ball!" As the audience applauds, my dad, Emily, and Manny come out onstage to join me. Chris introduces them as my family, so everyone probably thinks Manny is my brother, which is fine with me.

On the plane ride home, everybody tells me what a great job I did on **Better Than Sleeping!** and how well it went, and how we are going to sell a zillion more All Balls. I feel happy, but I'm also nervous.

Does that ever happen to you, where you feel two emotions at once? It's very complicated. How can you be happy and nervous at the same time? I don't know the answer to that, but I guess it's better than feeling happy and nauseated at the same time. Nervous and nauseated would be really terrible. I'm not so nervous that I feel nauseated, but I'm pretty close.

Why am I so nervous, you might be wondering? Tomorrow I start seventh grade. I'm a tiny bit nervous about that. But that's not it.

I have a secret about the All Ball that nobody knows, not even Manny.

And that secret has me feeling *really* nervous.

Chapter Three

Seventh Grade Begins

ALL SUMMER I FIGURED THAT THINGS WOULD BE A LITTLE different when school started, but as soon as I walk into the building, I realize just how different.

Some kids stare at me. Some point. Some act like they aren't looking at me, but their eyes dart in my direction. I hear kids whispering, "That's him!"

One tall guy I don't know yells, "Hey, Sure! Can I borrow a million dollars?" His friends laugh.

It is really weird. In sixth grade, Manny

and I were just regular kids, floating under the radar, trying not to get stuffed into lockers by the older kids. But now under the radar is totally over.

I find my locker and spin the lock, when a group of girls comes up to me. "You're Billy Sure?" one of them asks. I know her name. It's Allison. She was in my math class last year.

I nod my head.

"We saw you on that show," Allison says.

"Oh, great," I respond, not knowing what else to say.

"What's he like?" another girl asks a little breathlessly.

"Who?" I ask. "Chris Fernell? He's really nice."

The girl rolls her eyes. "No, not him. Dustin."

"Um, he seemed nice," I say, trying to remember something interesting about Dustin Peeler. "He gave my sister a soda."

The girls squeal with delight. "That is so Dustin!" Allison shrieks. "He cares so much!"

"If Dustin Peeler gave me a soda, I think I'd just die right on the spot," another girl says.

"And I'd never drink it," another adds. "I'd just keep it forever."

"It'd go flat," I say. "And it might get moldy."

The girls laugh like this is the funniest thing they've ever heard.

"He's cute," one of the girls whispers to her friends. "Almost as cute as Dustin." Then all the girls erupt into giggles.

Well, that's a first for me. I've never been called cute by a girl before. Except my mom, and she doesn't really count. I can feel my cheeks tingling and I know I'm blushing.

Lucky for me, the bell rings. **Brrrring!** The girls hurry off. "See you, Billy!" they call back to me as they go.

I round the corner to my homeroom before the second bell rings. It isn't hard to find, because there is a colorful banner hanging over the door that reads WELCOME, BILLY SURE!

Have you ever wished that the floor could

open up and swallow you, because you're so embarrassed? Yeah, that's exactly how I feel.

But the floor is not cooperating today, so I have no choice but to go to homeroom. It seems like everyone had been waiting for me to get here. When I walk in, a kid shouts, "He's here!" And then everyone starts clapping. I even hear someone whistle. I think it's Peter MacHale. He has a huge space between his two front teeth that he always tries to use to his advantage. You should see what he can do with bendy straws. My homeroom teacher, Mrs. Welch, smiles. "Congratulations on all your success over the summer, Billy! And welcome to my class!"

"Um, thanks," I mumble, and then I find a seat in the back of the room, wishing the whole time that Manny was in my homeroom. He would know how to handle this. But unfortunately we're in different homerooms this year. We don't even have any classes together. At least I have lunch to look forward to.

"Before we get started," Mrs. Welch says after I sit down, "I know we're all curious about the incredible summer Billy has had. Perhaps he'd like to tell us a little bit about his adventures as an inventor and a businessperson."

She smiles again and raises her eyebrows. Kids twist around in their seats, waiting for me to say something.

"Um, it's been pretty amazing," I say, because I can tell she wouldn't be happy if I said what I was thinking, which is, *No, thanks, I'm good just sitting here.* Mrs. Welch bobs her head up and down, and I realize I'm expected to say more. "Um, it's all kind of a jumble in my head. Maybe I could think about it and tell you some stuff later. Like, in a week or two. Or maybe a month."

Mrs. Welch looks a little disappointed, but she doesn't lose the smile. "That sounds fine, Billy." Not wanting to miss a potential teaching moment, she adds, "Preparation is a vital part of public speaking."

I hope that Mrs. Welch will be the only teacher who knows about the All Ball. Or at least the only teacher who makes a big deal out of it.

If only I could be that lucky. My first period is science, and it becomes clear pretty quickly that the teacher, Mr. Palnacchio, wants to talk about the All Ball too. We're barely settled into our seats when he tells us that we're going to start off the year with a unit on inventions. At first I think, *Cool, I should do really well on this unit.* And then as he talks more, I realize exactly what that means. "The very essence of science is curiosity. Discovery. Invention. But it's challenging. It takes a lot of hard work. So it's not often that you get to meet a success-ful inventor face to face," Mr. Palnacchio says dramatically, beaming at me.

UH-OH.

"But we're lucky today, class, because we have an extremely successful inventor right here in our own little science lab—Billy Sure!" He gestures toward me with an open palm, and I realize that, once again, I am expected to say something. But this time my mind goes com-pletely blank. So I do the only thing I can think of: I duck my head down and pretend to be really interested in some graffiti on my desk. After a few awkward moments of silence, Mr. Palnacchio seems to take the hint. "Well, more on that later, right, Billy?" he booms. "I have an idea I'll discuss with you right after class."

When the bell rings at the end of the period, I jump up to hurry to my next class, hoping Mr. Palnacchio forgot that he said he wanted to talk to me. But no such luck. He intercepts me at the door. "I was thinking we could plan the semester around an investigation of the

All Ball and how it works. We could cover mechanics, physics, even the chemistry of the materials and how they change! The students would love it! And for coteaching the class with me, you'd get lots of extra credit! What do you think, Billy?"

Think of a nice way to say no, I tell my brain. "It's an interesting idea, Mr. Palnacchio," I say slowly. "And you're right; there's some cool science behind the invention of the All Ball. . . ."

I take a breath. Mr. Palnacchio seems to be hanging on my every word, and the look on his face reminds me of the look my dog, Philo, gets on his face when he sees me reach into his treats jar. *You need to get to the "no" part,* I remind my brain.

". . . But I'm afraid the ball-morphing technology is patented, proprietary, and top secret," I say, thankful once again for Manny and his great ideas. "If I teach the class how it works, I'd get in a lot of trouble with the lawyers. And my business partner."

Mr. Palnacchio's face falls, and he nods. "Yes, that makes sense. I understand that you can't reveal your secrets." Then he brightens. "But think about it! I'm sure there's a way you could teach some of the general principles you've mastered without giving any secrets away!"

"Okay, Mr. Palnacchio. I will think about it," I promise, but not because I really want to. Right now I just want to leave. "Can I get to my next class now?"

As I jog down the hallway, I see a kid at the other end of the hall coming straight toward me. He locks eyes with me.

He's a big kid. A really big kid.

I think about turning around and going the other way, but the huge guy is already right in front of me. With those long legs, the entire hallway is only about three steps for him.

"You Billy Sure?" he snarls.

I consider making up a fake name on the spot, like McCallister Snifferton.

I look around for help. The hall is empty. Where is everyone?

"Yeah," I admit. "I'm Billy Sure."

"The guy that invented the All Ball?" he growls in his low, bearlike voice.

I nod, wondering if I will be able to block his punches with my backpack.

Maybe this bully is a mind reader, because right then he reaches into *his* backpack. What is he going to pull out? A rock? A club? Nunchucks?

No. He pulls out an All Ball.

"Would you mind signing this for me?" he asks.

A wave of relief washes over me. "Of course not!" I squeak as I pull a pen out of my pocket. "Who should I make it out to?"

"Dudley. Dudley Dillworthy," he says.

He takes his signed All Ball and runs off to class.

By the time I get to lunch, I am wishing I'd asked Dudley to be my bodyguard. In the cafeteria, kids mob around me and Manny, asking us to sit with them. The table we end up at is so crowded, there is barely any room to sit. I have never felt so much pressure eating before. With everyone staring at me, I have to be careful with every bite. I'm usually the last one to know when I have mustard on my nose or poppy seeds in my teeth. As a best friend, it's Manny's job to tell me these things, but he never notices. Right now he's huddled over his phone, probably making some new business deal for the All Ball.

"Hey, Sure," one of the boys at my table blurts out. His name is Jeff. I look down at my shirt, thinking that Jeff is going to tell me that I'm wearing some applesauce.

"How much money do you have?" Jeff asks.

A hush comes over the cafeteria as everyone waits for my answer, even the cafeteria ladies. I see one of them pause with a big ladle in her hand, waiting until after I speak to finish slopping soup in a bowl.

"I don't really know," I admit. "For now, most of the money goes right back into the company. When a company's new, there are lots of expenses. My parents are handling any money that comes to me, putting it in a bank account for college."

I hear sighs. I see frowns. Nobody likes this answer. It's boring, but it's the truth.

"But I heard you carry, like, a thousand bucks in your wallet," Jeff claims.

"I heard ten thousand," shouts someone else.

I shake my head. "I don't think a thousand bucks would fit in my wallet. I don't really know. I've never seen a thousand dollars."

Then everyone in the cafeteria starts arguing about whether a thousand dollars would fit in a wallet, and whether there is a one-thousand-dollar bill. A sixth grader boasts that she held one in her hands, and then her friends tell her that she's a big liar. Which is good, because it takes the attention away from me for a couple of minutes.

I finish my lunch as fast as I can and get out of there.

In English the teacher assigns an essay on "WHAT I INVENTED THIS SUMMER." In social studies the teacher suggests we discuss "the economics of sports, especially new sports technologies." In gym the teacher pulls me aside and asks if Sure Things, Inc. could donate a bunch of All Balls to the school. "It'd really help us out," he pleads. "The budget cuts have been brutal! When we need new nets for the basketball hoops, my wife has to knit them!"

Late that afternoon there's an announcement. "Will Billy Sure please report to the principal's office?"

Why do they always summon you to the principal's office in the form of a question? Are you allowed to say no? *Sorry, but I really can't come to the principal's office right now. Or ever.*

I reluctantly trudge down to the office. I wonder what I did wrong. Am I going to be suspended for disrupting classes with my fame? Given detention for inspiring the teachers to give us crazy assignments?

When I walk in, the secretary behind the counter smiles at me and says, "Hi, Billy. Mr. Gilamon is waiting for you."

It seems like a good sign that the secretary smiled at me, right? I mean, would she smile at a kid who was about to get detention? Unless that's part of her job. Maybe they tell her she has to smile at everyone who comes in, even the kids who are in REALLY BIG TROUBLE.

But when I enter Mr. Gilamon's office, he shoots up out of his chair, steps around his desk, and shakes my hand, smiling broadly. "Billy Sure! Congratulations on your success! Well done!"

"Thanks," I mumble. "Um, am I in trouble?"

Mr. Gilamon gives a big hearty laugh. "No! Just the opposite! From what I hear, you're in the catbird's seat!"

I have no idea what that means, but as long as it doesn't mean "detention," I'm okay with it.

Motioning for me to have a seat (not a catbird's, just a regular seat), the principal sits back down in his big chair. "Billy, I think what you've done, inventing the, uh . . . what's it called?"

"The All Ball."

"Right! The All Ball! Inventing the All Ball, and starting your own company, and having so much success, is incredibly inspirational. It's just the kind of thing we need here at Fillmore Middle School to inspire our students. And future students! Just think, someday students will say, 'Billy Sure went to my school!'"

I hadn't thought of that. That is pretty cool.

Mr. Gilamon makes a little tent with his fingers. "I want to make sure every student in this school is aware of your inspiring achievement. It could spark a tidal wave of excellence!"

I'm not sure how a tidal wave could start with a spark, but I don't point that out to the principal.

"Now, Billy, let me ask you something," he continues. "When's your birthday?"

I didn't see that coming. Does he want to buy me a present?

"March twenty-eighth," I reply. "Why?" I suddenly think of something horrible. "You're not going to make me skip a grade, are you? Because I really don't want to."

He laughs his booming laugh again. "No, no! I just had an idea that we'd make your birthday a special holiday here at Fillmore Middle School."

"You mean we'd get the day off?" I ask. That'd be pretty sweet. Everyone would love me for that.

"Uh, no, not that kind of holiday," he says quickly.

What's the point of having a holiday if you can't get a day off from school for it?

"This would be a celebration of your birthday, honoring your achievement and inspiring other kids to reach for their own dreams!" he says enthusiastically. He looks up at the calendar on his wall, which has a picture of a guy climbing a mountain, and adds "Do what you've always dreamed of doing." That makes me think of swinging so high that I loop around the swing set. I've dreamed of doing that since kindergarten. I've never even gotten close. It

might not be possible, but I'll keep trying until I'm too big to sit on a swing.

I look up at Mr. Gilamon. He's still talking. "But March is a long way off. I was hoping we could inspire the students right at the beginning of the school year. You wouldn't consider changing your birthday, would you?"

I don't know what to say, so I open my mouth. Maybe something will come out and surprise me. I make an "uh" sound. Principal Gilamon laughs as though I'd made the most hilarious joke he'd ever heard.

"Well, maybe we could have a celebration

that wasn't actually on your birthday," he says. "BILLY SURE DAY!"

I don't think I really needed *more* attention at school. "How about just calling it Invention Day?" I suggest. "Or Achievement Day? Or Reach For Your Dreams Day?"

Mr. Gilamon grabs a pad and a pen and starts writing furiously. "Those are all great suggestions!" he says. "Billy, you're full of ideas! No wonder you're so successful!"

When the last bell of the day rings, I launch out of my seat so fast that my math teacher gives me a look. I smile apologetically as I bolt out the door. The first day of seventh grade has been really strange, but at least it's over.

"So, how was the rest of your day?" Manny asks as we head out the door together.

I shrug. Where do I even start?

Manny smiles. "You can tell me all about it at the office."

Chapter Four

The Office

THE OFFICE OF SURE THINGS, INC. ISN'T IN SOME TALL building downtown. It's the garage at Manny's house. His parents generously let us take it over to use as the headquarters of Sure Things, Inc.

Maybe Manny's parents are willing to park their cars on the street because Manny's an only child. He gets away with a lot more than I do. Plus he doesn't have to deal with Emily. On some days, I really envy him. Make that most days.

It used to be just a regular garage—car smell,

oil stains on the floor, dark—but since the All Ball took off, we've made a lot of changes. Sure, there's normal office stuff, which is kinda boring, but I think Manny really likes what he picked out for chairs, lamps, and computers. But what I love about the office are the extras. It's the kind of hideout I always dreamed of having, and now I have it, which is pretty cool.

There's a state-of-the-art soda machine with a digital display that lets you mix custom flavors. Manny once calculated how many possible flavors there are. I forget the exact total he came up with, but I'm pretty sure it was in the millions. Although most of the combinations are things you'd probably never want to drink, like PICKLE-GRAPE-BANANA-COLA. Actually, now that I think about it, I kind of want to taste that flavor. *Remember to try that flavor sometime,* I tell my brain. The machine even has a mystery flavor. We still haven't figured out what it is.

Then, to go with your soda, there's pizza. We have this machine that dispenses hot slices.

Enter the toppings you want, press a button, and a perfectly cooked slice of hot pizza comes sliding out. And like our soda machine, Manny and I made sure there are some crazy flavor combos. You can put chocolate chips on your pizza or use peanut butter instead of tomato sauce. The craziest slice we've come up with so far had graham cracker crust, soy sauce, shredded coconut instead of cheese, and jalapeño peppers on top. Neither of us was brave enough to actually try it, but it was fun to create.

It's really great having so many food options at the office, because my father thinks he's a gourmet cook, but he's completely wrong about that. Lately he's been trying to master something he calls beets à l'orange. Emily calls it BLECH À LA YUCK.

We can't always work nonstop in the office, so we've also got a pitching machine for batting practice, a basketball hoop, and a punching bag. (We tell people those are for testing out the All Ball. Well, not the punching bag. That's for punching.) Oh, and every video game console ever made, going back to the eight-bit systems that my dad used to play. Thank you, Internet!

And a pinball machine. And foosball. And air hockey.

Actually, we're thinking about getting rid of the desks.

Oh, and probably the most important feature of the office is Philo (named after Philo T. Farnsworth, the inventor who helped make TV possible). Philo has shaggy brown hair and big brown eyes. He's technically my family's dog, but I think of him as *my* dog because I'm pretty sure I'm his favorite person. I think Emily's mood swings are a bit much for him, and he learned the hard way to steer clear of my dad when he's in the kitchen. Philo loves hanging out in the office with me and Manny. He even has his own doggy bed in the corner. Philo's

the unofficial mascot of Sure Things, Inc.

The first thing I do when Manny and I arrive at the office today after school is dispense myself a slice and a raspberry-ginger root beer while I tell Manny about the rest of my day.

"My day was pretty strange too," Manny says when I'm done. "Everyone kept asking about you, and how much money you have now, and whether you were interested in giving some to them."

"What did you say?"

"I told them we were broke," he says, laughing. As we talk, Manny tosses a small All Ball from one hand to the other. I hold the unit's remote, hitting a button every time the ball reaches the top of its arc, changing it before it falls into Manny's hand. From tennis ball to baseball to golf ball to hockey puck to Ping-Pong ball and back to tennis ball . . .

Manny never drops the ball.

"Hey!" he says suddenly. "I haven't checked All Ball sales in over three hours!" He sets down the small All Ball and turns to his laptop. Manny loves to review sales figures and see them going up. But it isn't about the money for him. He hardly ever *spends* any money, other than what we spent decking out the office. He just loves big numbers and setting records. It's like he has a collection he's obsessed with, only his collection isn't stamps or pencil toppers, but sales figures.

I decide to check my e-mail. Once Manny starts looking at sales figures, there's no talking to him until he's done.

There's an e-mail from my mom:

Hi, Billy,

How are you doing? How's business? And school, of course? What new inventions are you working on? I'm super busy just now, so I can't write a long e-mail, but I wanted you to know I'm thinking about you and I love you.

Love,

Mom

P.S. Please note my new e-mail address. The old one got hacked, so I had to change it.

I hit reply right away.

Hi, Mom!

Today was the first day of school. It was crazy. Everyone wanted to talk to me about the All Ball, even Principal Gilamon! The Hyenas are doing great. Well, not really, but Carl Bourette hit an in-the-park home run during the last game. I was shouting so loud that Emily threatened to duct-tape my mouth shut.

That reminds me. I had a great idea for a new invention that you can eat when your mouth isn't covered in tape. It's Mud Pie Seasoning, and it'll turn regular mud pies into delicious desserts. What do you think?

Write back soon.

Love,

Billy

After I send the e-mail, I think about how much I miss my mom. It's not the same watching Hyena games without her. Dad and

Emily aren't interested in baseball, but Mom loves it. She says that watching the games with me helps her relax. Since my mom left at the beginning of July, she's missed a lot of games this year.

Eventually, Manny stops looking at his laptop and turns back to me. "So," he asks. "What's next?"

"Another slice of pizza?" I suggest. "I'm thinking of adding jelly beans to this one, but I'm not sure."

"No," Manny says, getting up and wandering over to the foosball table to give one of the rods a spin. "I mean what's next for Sure Things, Inc.? The All Ball's doing great, but we don't want to be a one-product company."

That's Manny. Always thinking about the business stuff. It's a good thing he likes the business side, because it doesn't interest me all that much. I'm much more interested in inventions. I have been since I was a little kid. My mom says that when I was a baby, I invented a new use for diapers (throwing them), but I don't think that counts.

"You mean like a new invention?" I ask.

"Exactly," Manny says.

"How about MUD PIE SEASONING?" I suggest. "Mud pies can finally taste like pie pies."

Manny thinks about it and then frowns. "But who would want to eat dirt?" he says. "No, we need something bigger. And less disgusting."

We both sit there thinking. I start messing with the air hockey table, spinning a puck on its edge. Manny wanders over to a chess set, stares at it a minute, and moves the black knight. He's playing a match against himself, which I don't get at all. I mean, how can you play chess when black knows exactly what white's going to do, and vice versa?

"What about the CANDY BRUSH?" Manny asks as he sits down behind his desk.

Ah, the Candy Brush! The first invention I ever told Manny about. It was the first day of first grade. I'd thought of the Candy Brush that morning when my mom forced me to brush my teeth before school, and I couldn't wait to tell someone about it. At recess I spotted Manny standing by himself, so I blurted out my idea and he liked it. We've been friends ever since.

"I still haven't really cracked that one yet," I admit. The idea for the Candy Brush is that it would make ordinary toothpaste taste like candy. It'd make kids run into the bathroom to brush their teeth after every meal!

"The sweet and sour angle is key," Manny says, drumming his fingers on the desk. Manny thinks we should sell two different kinds of Candy Brush. One would make toothpaste taste like sweet candy, while the other would make toothpaste taste like sour candy. Manny figures kids would want to have both, so we'd double our sales.

With another product Manny would have a whole new set of sales figures to obsess over. He'd be so happy.

We talk about the Candy Brush some more,

but I remind him again that I haven't figured out exactly how to make it work. Manny looks disappointed, so I suggest that we should keep thinking about what our next product will be. Maybe there's an even better idea out there. Manny reluctantly agrees. He really loves the Candy Brush idea. I think he wants one for himself. He hates toothpaste.

When Philo and I get home, I can smell Dad's cooking. Yeech. "I'm adding a new ingredient to my beets à l'orange!" he calls from the kitchen. "Kale!"

Emily sticks her finger in her mouth, making a gagging gesture. Then she sees me, and her eyes narrow. "Thanks for ruining my life."

"How did I ruin your life? I thought you were taking care of that yourself."

"My very first day of high school and all anyone asks me about is you and your stupid All Ball," she says. "Everyone wants to know how much money you have, and if my family is rich now, and if we're going to buy a summer house, and if they can come to our summer house and spend the night. Or the summer."

I shrug. "That doesn't sound so bad. At least people are talking to you. And you didn't seem to think the All Ball was so stupid when Dustin Peeler was playing with it."

She snorts. "Dustin Peeler. I'm totally over him."

"How can you be over him?" I ask, amazed. "You were completely in love with him, like, thirty-six hours ago! Did he do something?"

"Yes," she says. "He played with your stupid All Ball!"

She stomps off to her room.

I manage to eat a little bit of Dad's dinner, watch some TV, and do my homework. (I can't believe we already have homework on the very first day!) Philo gets into his bed in my room, and I get into mine. "Good night, Philo," I say. He sighs, snuggles down, and quickly falls asleep.

I lie there staring at the framed blueprints on my wall.

They're the original blueprints for the All

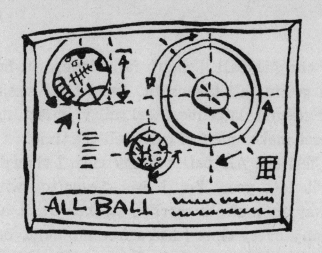

Ball—the diagram showing how to make my amazing invention.

I didn't really want the blueprints hanging on my bedroom wall, but my parents were so proud of me that they gave the framed blueprints to me as a surprise. My dad even made the frame (he's an artist, so he knows all about frames). What could I do? Take them down and slide them under the bed?

So now I find myself staring at them every night before I fall asleep. And I'm always thinking the same thing . . .

Where did they come from?

That's my secret. I didn't draw the blueprints

for the All Ball. I didn't fully invent it, but I'm getting all the credit. Every time someone congratulates me, I feel guilty. In fact, my secret makes me feel guilty all the time.

Yes, the All Ball was my idea. I thought of it last year. But I was struggling with a way to make it work. I worked on it all spring, every time I had a free moment. But I just couldn't crack it. I was getting close, but there were still a few crucial details I was stuck on.

Then one morning in June I woke up and found the blueprints on my desk. They were perfect. They solved every problem I'd been wrestling with. I was so excited, I ran to Manny's house with the blueprints and we got to work right away.

I never told him that the blueprints just appeared on my desk. He was so excited, and I didn't want to let him down. I thought whoever left the blueprints would fess up soon, but it's been months now and I still don't know who put them there.

Dad? He's an artist, so he could draw a really good set of blueprints. But he's never invented anything in his life, as far as I know.

Mom? She's a researcher, and really smart, so maybe she could figure it out. But why wouldn't she tell me?

Emily? No way. She'd definitely want to take credit for figuring out how to make the All Ball.

A ghost?

I thought about asking my family members, but it sounded so weird in my head. "Hey, did you figure out how to make the All Ball and draw up blueprints and put them on my desk but then forget to tell me you did it?" It sounds crazy.

But how did they get there?

Chapter Five

The Flying Phone

WHEN I WAKE UP THE NEXT MORNING, I HOPE THAT ON the second day of seventh grade things will be a little more normal and everyone will be over staring at me and making such a big deal out of everything. But that's not what happens.

"Hey, Billy!" I hear from behind a tree on my walk to school. At first I think I must be hallucinating. Trees are trying to talk to me?

But then a boy from my homeroom pops out from behind it. His name is Steve Stallings. I don't know Steve well, but I do know that in gym class last year Steve fell during a game of kickball and dislocated his knee. His kneecap was on his thigh. It was weird and scary and cool at the same time.

"What's up?" I reply to Steve. I notice that Steve's kneecap has made it back to its correct position.

"Not much," he says. We walk almost a block in silence.

"So," he says, "you're an inventor."

"Yeah."

"So am I."

"Cool," I say. We walk a little farther.

"Don't you want to know what I invented?" he asks, sounding a little annoyed.

"Um, sure. What did you invent?"

Steve smiles. Then he looks around, checking to see if anyone is eavesdropping on us, before he tells me about his invention.

"THE FLYING PHONE," he whispers.

"Oh," I say. "What's a flying phone?"

"Not so loud!" he says in a loud whisper. He looks around again, and then I guess he feels satisfied that no one can hear us so he speaks

in a normal voice. "It's a phone that flies!"

"Yeah, I kinda figured that. But why?"

"Why what?"

I stop walking and face him. He stops too. "Why would you want a flying phone? What would you do with it?"

"Well," he says. "Let's say your phone is ringing, but you're on the other side of the room. After a few rings, these wings pop out on the side of the phone. Then the phone flies over to you."

"Huh," I say, walking again. "It seems like you could just walk across the room and get your phone."

Steve frowns and I suddenly feel bad. I don't want to dash Steve's dreams. It's just that inventors have to really ask themselves why people would want their invention—that's the first thing I do when I come up with an idea. The second thing I do is try to come up with a cool name for my invention. Steve had come up with a cool name for his invention, at least. "Can I see it?" I ask.

"Oh, I haven't made one," Steve replies. "That's where you come in."

"What's a flying phone got to do with me?"

"You'll figure out how to make it, and then your company will produce it. Since it was my idea, I'll get ninety percent of the money we make," Steve explains.

"Or possibly eighty percent," he says after a minute of my silence. "It's negotiable. To a certain extent."

"I'll think about it," I tell Steve as we walk into homeroom. Steve huffs off to his seat.

At least the WELCOME, BILLY SURE! banner has been taken down. That's a relief.

But before I can get to my seat, Mrs. Welch waves me over. "So," she asks quietly, "have you started working on your speech?"

I don't know what she's talking about. "Speech?"

"About your adventures over the summer!" she

explains. "As an inventor! And a businessperson!"

Oh, right. I completely forgot about that. "I'm thinking about it," I say. "Getting my thoughts organized."

She smiles and nods, as though we're sharing a secret. "Very good! Well, I look forward to it. And I'm sure your fellow students do too."

In science class Mr. Palnacchio takes me aside too, wanting to talk more about which lessons I might be willing to teach. "Now, I know you can't reveal any secrets about the All Ball, but based on the way it changes color, I was thinking you might like to teach the Science of Color unit," he suggests. "After all, I thought I understood color science, but I have *no idea* how you get the ball to change from white to brown to orange. Fascinating!"

I love science, but I can't teach a class in it. What if some of my classmates started goofing around? How would I get them to stop? I'd rather be goofing around myself. I tell Mr. Palnacchio I'm not really sure about helping him teach the class, but I'll keep thinking about it.

It seems as though the teachers are determined to give me lots of things to think about. As if I don't already have plenty to think about.

At lunch more kids come up to me with their ideas for inventions, all of them hoping to make millions of dollars. Here are some of their ideas:

- A knife that comes prepackaged with peanut butter and jelly in the handle.
- Shoes that can change from sneakers to flip-flops to dress shoes with the touch of a button. (I think maybe the All Ball inspired that one.)
- Flying skateboards. (Pretty sure they saw that one in a movie.)
- A device you can hide in your mouth that turns you into a great singer.

No one other than Manny ever used to be interested in talking with me about inventions. But now that I've had a successful one, *everyone* wants to talk to me about inventions! I can't get them to talk about anything else! I like talking about inventions, but not all the time.

By the end of the day I feel lousy, like the time Manny dared me to ride the MegaCoaster seventeen times in a row. My guilt over not really inventing the All Ball is making me feel even worse than the MegaCoaster did. (By the way, I was only able to ride it thirteen times before I threw up. And after that they wouldn't let me back on the ride.)

I can't take it anymore. I need to talk to Manny.

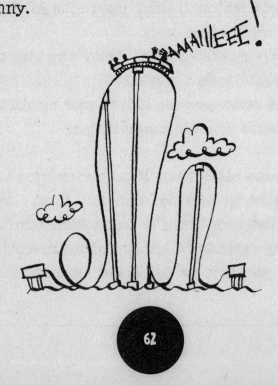

Chapter Six

The Next Big Thing

WHEN PHILO AND I GET TO THE OFFICE, MANNY'S ALREADY there. I smell pizza. Manny is eating a slice.

"Sales figures look good," Manny says, staring at his computer. "Especially South America. Which is a little surprising, since I thought they only loved to play soccer down there."

Philo sniffs around, then settles into his bed in the corner. I hit the punching bag. *Whap!* "Manny, we need to talk."

"I'm pretty sure that's what we're doing right now," he says, still staring at his computer.

I sit down next to him. "No, we need to

really talk. About something important."

Manny finally looks up from his screen, surprised. "What could possibly be more important than sales figures?"

"The whole thing," I say, spreading my arms open. "I want to talk about the whole thing."

He's confused. "What whole thing?" Then he looks excited. "Is that your next invention? THE HOLE THING? Does it fix holes, like in pants? Or buckets? What about holes in hoses? There are so many possibilities!"

I shake my head. "No, it's not my next invention. I mean this whole business thing. Sure Things, Inc."

Manny looks worried. "What about it?"

I take a deep breath. "I'm not sure I can handle all this. It was okay over the summer, but now with school and people coming up to me all the time, it's too much."

Manny looks relieved. He picks up a small All Ball and starts tossing it up, letting it fall, and catching it. He tosses it almost all the way up to the ceiling of the garage. I'm tempted to secretly change the ball with the remote, but we're having a serious conversation.

"You probably just need a few days to adjust," Manny says. "Today was only the second day of school. It'll get better."

"Will it?" I ask, getting up and pacing around. "I thought *today* would be better. That everyone would've gotten over it and start obsessing over something else. Like how Mr. Frankenwald shaved the shape of a chicken into his buzz cut over the summer."

Manny laughs, thinking about the sixth-grade art teacher's new haircut. "Yeah, not sure what he's going for there."

"But today even *more* kids asked me questions!" I continue. "Everyone wants to talk to

me about their ideas for inventions. It never stops. I don't know if I want to do this anymore. Can't we just do it later, when we're older?"

Manny looks alarmed. He obviously doesn't want to just put the business on hold. "Billy, lots of people are depending on Sure Things now. They're working for the company, and it's their job. You can't just take their jobs away! And who knows if people will still buy the All Ball later. Things change! Fast!"

"Yeah, I noticed," I say, thinking of how my life has changed over the summer.

Manny thinks for a minute.

"You know, people telling you their ideas, that part doesn't really sound all that bad."

I think about it. "I guess you're right. It's fun hearing other people's ideas, but I just don't want them interrupting me all the time."

Manny nods. "That makes sense. I can see how that could start to drive you crazy. Maybe next time someone starts bugging you, you can think of a way to let them down easy. It never hurts to stand up for yourself."

He walks over to his chessboard and moves a white bishop. He smiles. Then he walks around to the other side of the board and frowns. I guess it was a good move for white and a bad move for black.

He looks up. "Let me think about it. Maybe there's something we can do to make things better for you. In the meantime, don't give up on Sure Things just yet. And keep thinking about a way to make the Candy Brush work! I still think that's a great idea."

He sits back down at his computer, so I wake up mine and check my e-mail. There's one from my mom:

Hi, Billy,
    Wow. Mud Pie Seasoning. Cool idea. What other inventions are you working on? I'd love to hear more about how your business is going. Tell me all about it! When you do, send me lots of details. That way it doesn't seem as though we're so far apart.

Love,
Mom
P.S. Go, Hyenas!

I reply right away, telling her about how I'm working on the Candy Brush. Then I write about the Hyenas' chances of making the play-offs, even though their chances are pretty much zilch minus zero. Same as every other year.

By lunchtime the next day I'm beginning to think that things are getting a little better. I only got five loan requests this morning. Other than the kid who followed me into the bathroom to beg me to invent jet packs, it's been a pretty normal day.

Then I hear the announcement over the loudspeaker. "Will Billy Sure please report to the principal's office?"

"Ooh!" say all the kids around me, assuming I'm in big trouble, especially because this is the second time I've been called down there in three

o-o=definitely

days. Maybe this time I really am in trouble.

As I walk as slowly as possible through the halls, I think about the announcement: "Will Billy Sure please report to the principal's office?" Why do they always say "report?" Am I supposed to walk in with pages in a binder? Ready to give a speech on *Huckleberry Finn* or the Greek gods? You never "report" to anything good. *"Please report to the carnival." "Please report to the water park." "Please report to your birthday party."*

When I sit down in Principal Gilamon's office, it's pretty obvious I'm not in trouble, because he's got a huge smile on his face. "Billy!" he says. "Just the man I want to see!" He says this as though I just dropped into his office to surprise him, not because I was summoned over a loudspeaker.

"I want to show you something," he says. "I think you're going to like it."

He reaches behind his desk and holds up a poster. Across the top it says, *You'd better believe you're gonna achieve!* There are lots of stars and rainbows and fireworks. And the bottom two-thirds of

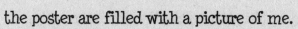

the poster are filled with a picture of me.

As if that's not bad enough, it's not even a good picture of me. It's my school picture from sixth grade. The photographer was trying to make me smile, so he stuck his tongue out. But instead of smiling, I look weirded out.

So even though the poster says, *You'd better believe you're gonna achieve!,* in the picture I look like I don't believe it for a second.

I'm not sure what to say.

"Well," Principal Gilamon says, "what do you think?"

"What's it for?"

"It's our poster for Achievement Day!" he says. "Week after next, we're going to have a day dedicated to achievement. And I was hoping you might be willing to give an inspirational speech to your fellow students."

"What would I say?"

He chuckles. "Well, I was hoping you'd talk about your own achievements with the Everything Ball—"

"All Ball."

"Right, the All Ball, and about some of the qualities it took for you to reach that achievement—drive, discipline, dedication ... hey! Those all start with *D*! That could be your speech! The Three *D*s! Or you could call it Achieving in 3-D! We could hand out 3-D glasses! Oh, this is great!"

He starts scribbling down ideas on a big pad of paper. He looks so enthusiastic that I hate to burst his bubble.

But I have to. I take a deep breath and then the words just start tumbling out of my mouth.

"Mr. Gilamon, I'm finding all the attention I'm getting really distracting. It makes it hard for me to concentrate on my schoolwork and my ... work work. I've got a lot on my mind. If I had to write a speech to deliver in front of the whole school, I think I'd go crazy. Achievement

Day sounds like an okay idea, but I don't want my picture on the poster. And I don't want to give a speech. I kind of wish I could just be a normal student that day, instead of the one everyone's staring at and wanting to be like or borrow money from or punch."

I stop speaking and take another breath.

Mr. Gilamon looks concerned. "Has anyone punched you?"

"No," I say. "Actually, everyone's been pretty nice. But I'm afraid giving a speech might make some of them want to punch me."

The principal sits there for a moment, thinking. Then he smiles and nods. "I understand, Billy. Of course I don't want to do anything that'll interfere with your schoolwork—that's the most important thing. And I don't want to make you uncomfortable."

He stands up. So do I.

"Maybe we'll just put Achievement Day on hold for now," he says. "Don't worry about it. It sounds as though you've already got plenty to think about."

Whew. Principal Gilamon is actually a really cool guy.

After school, when I get to the office with Philo, Manny's excited. "I think I've got a solution to your problem."

"Which one?"

"The one where everybody wants to tell you their ideas for new inventions."

"Headphones? Bodyguards? A force field surrounding me at all times?"

Manny actually considers my last suggestion for a second. "Interesting," he says. "Personal force fields. I like it. Maybe it could shoot out of your belt or something. We could call it the AVOID STUFF BELT—"

"But what's your idea?" I interrupt.

"The Internet," he says proudly.

"But, Manny, the Internet already exists."

Manny paces around, moving his hands through his dark hair. He does that when he's excited. Philo follows him, but he doesn't even notice.

"We're not inventing the Internet, but putting something on it. We'll make a website called SURE THINGS' NEXT BIG THING! Kids who have ideas for inventions will be able to upload videos explaining their ideas."

"Okay," I say. "Then what?"

"Then if you and I like any of the ideas, we'll e-mail the inventor and ask if he or she would like Sure Things, Inc. to take the idea and develop it. We manufacture the product and share the profits with the inventor. And we hope each product will be the next big thing!"

"So, a website for kids' ideas for inventions," I say, thinking about Manny's idea.

"I figure it'll take some of the pressure off you to come up with ideas for more inventions like the All Ball," Manny says.

But I'll still have the pressure of actually *developing* the inventions. And Manny still doesn't know I'm not the one who solved the problem of how to make the All Ball. Every day that I don't confess only makes it worse. But every time I think about it, I chicken out.

I need some bravery serum or something. If I couldn't figure out how to make my own idea work, how will I be able to figure out somebody else's idea?

But I don't tell Manny what I'm thinking. Instead I ask, "And how does this solve my problem of kids coming up to me at school and telling me their ideas for inventions?"

Manny grins and hands me a business card. "If anyone comes up to you and starts explaining their brilliant idea, you just give them one of these."

I look at the card. It says *Sure Things' Next Big Thing!* Underneath there's a web address.

"Well," Manny says impatiently. "What do you think? Genius, huh?"

I'm not totally sure about the idea. I mean, I know it's brilliant, but the pressure of having to figure out a way to develop all of these inventions is a serious problem. But Manny's so enthusiastic about his idea that I say yes. Who knows? Maybe no one will submit any ideas anyway.

Chapter Seven

Motor Beds and Super Sleds

BOY, WAS I WRONG.

Manny gets the website up and running quickly. Then he goes through all the media contacts—television reporters, magazine writers, website editors—that he collected when everyone wanted to do stories about the All Ball. I'm pretty sure he even has celebrities like Dustin Peeler and Carl Bourette on his list of contacts. He sends them a press release about Sure Things' Next Big Thing, and the word spreads.

QUICKLY.

In no time at all, we're getting so many videos from kids all over the world that the website crashes. Even though Manny makes the rules really clear (kids only, original ideas only, useful inventions only), there are still tons of videos.

At the office, sipping multiflavored sodas, Manny and I start watching the videos together, taking notes on our computers.

One of the first videos that arrives on the website is from a kid in Canada. He's standing in his bedroom, waving at his computer's camera.

"Hello!" he says. "My name is Mark, and I'd like to tell you my idea for Sure Things' Next Big Thing!"

Mark jumps onto his bed. "Has this ever happened to you? You're lying in bed, snuggled under the covers. You're warm. You're cozy. You're happy!"

Mark gets under the covers and pulls them up to his chin, looking very warm and cozy indeed.

"But then your mom yells, 'MARK! HURRY UP! YOU HAVE TO GO TO YOUR PIANO LESSON!'" Mark screams this part in a high-pitched voice. Then he speaks in his normal voice again. "Now you have to get out of your nice, cozy bed. *Or do you?!*"

Mark gets out of his bed and approaches the camera. "Not if you have a motor for your bed! Just attach a motor to your bed and then you can drive it anywhere. You'll never have to get out of your warm, cozy bed again!"

Mark moves even closer to his computer, reaching to shut it off. I can see up his nostrils. I wish I couldn't. "Thank you for your attention. Please help me make the MOTOR BED Sure Things' Next Big Thing."

Manny turns to me. "Hey! That's not a bad idea."

"Definitely. Is there anyone who loves getting out of bed when you're all snuggled up under the covers?" I say. "But I see one major problem."

"What's that?"

"Doors. How would you get through them? We'd either have to make larger doors or smaller beds. It's too complicated."

"Good point," Manny agrees. "Next."

In the next video a girl holds up a sock. "I present the NO-WASH SOCK! I've come up with a material that's so slick, dirt can't stick to it. So your socks always look nice and clean!"

She moves a little closer to the camera. "But I could use your help with two small problems. One, the socks are so slick, they slide around in your shoes. Two, even though they *look* clean, these socks still start to smell after not being washed for a week or two."

Manny and I laugh. "So they're clean, but they're hard to wear and they stink!" he says.

"I think we'll put that in the 'no' pile," I say.

"Or the dirty laundry pile," Manny adds.

He clicks on another video. This one's from a kid all the way in Finland.

"Hello!" he says, standing outdoors and waving. "My name is Franz. Tired of your plain old sled? Then why not try **FRANZ'S SUPER SLED**! Like a regular sled, Franz's Super Sled slides down snowy hills. But it slides super fast!"

Then the video cuts to a shot of Franz at the top of a hill. He waves, pulls goggles down over his eyes, gets on the sled, and pushes off. **Zoom! Crash!**

Manny and I grimace as we watch the sled zoom down the hill as fast as a cheetah flying a jet plane and then crash into the snowbank at the bottom of the hill.

"I'm okay!" Franz calls as he climbs out of the snow.

"*Snow* way on that invention," says Manny, laughing at his little joke. "Too dangerous."

The ideas just keep coming.

A boy submits an idea for a pencil that does all your homework for you, although the prototype keeps going rogue and scribbling all over his walls and even his parents. Too many bugs to work out.

A girl suggests bubble gum that's stretchy enough that you can blow bubbles as big as hot air balloons. But when a bubble pops, it covers the chewer in gum goo. The inventor had to shave all her hair off. Too sticky.

We watch another video about shoes that can take over for your legs, allowing you to run incredibly fast and jump incredibly high. I think that idea sounds really cool, but Manny quickly points out that it's way too dangerous.

Manny and I watch so many videos that I feel like I need a new pair of eyeballs, they hurt so much. We start to see ideas more than once. It's amazing that even though two kids live on opposite sides of the planet, they both come up with the same idea about pants with springs in them so you can bounce on your butt.

"My 'no' column is a lot longer than my 'maybe' column," I tell Manny.

"Mine too, but that's good," Manny replies. "We don't need thousands of ideas. In fact, we really only need one terrific one."

We keep watching until we feel as though our eyes are going to fall out of our skulls. Many of the videos are too dark, or too light, or out of focus. Sometimes the person steps out of the picture, so you're just staring at a wall. A lot of times the audio is hard to understand. But while we're watching all these videos, more keep arriving. And more. And more. Just keeping track of which ones we've watched is hard enough.

"Help," Manny moans.

"What's the matter?"

"No, I mean we need help," he explains. "We

can't spend all our time watching these videos from the website. I've got other things to do."

"Okay," I say, nodding. "But where are we going to get help? Who can we get to watch all these videos for us? Philo? He has kind of a short attention span."

Hearing his name, Philo looks up from his doggy bed. When he realizes I'm not giving him a treat, he plops his head back down.

"I've got an idea about who we can get," Manny says.

"No way, genius," Emily says, making the kind of face she usually reserves for Dad's stuffed sardines. "I have no interest in hanging out with you and your math whiz buddy in a hot, smelly garage."

I am standing in my sister's bedroom, pleading my case while she lies on her bed putting polish on her toenails. Black polish, of course.

"It's not hot," I protest. "It's air-conditioned. We have to keep it cool for the computers. And it's not smelly, either. I mean, a lot of the time it smells like pizza, but that's not smelly. That's delicious." I wrinkle my nose. "Nail polish is *way* stinkier than our office."

"Forget it," she says. "Close the door as you go."

I have an idea. "You know, you wouldn't have to work in our office. You can watch the videos and take notes on them anywhere. Then you can e-mail us your notes. And who knows? You might be part of a really important new technology! One that changes the world!"

"You mean like stinky, uncomfortable socks?"

I wish I hadn't talked about that at dinner. I decide to try a new tactic.

"You know, Manny is trying to get Dustin

Peeler to sing a jingle for an All Ball commercial. If he does it, maybe we could arrange for you to meet him again."

"I already told you, I'm not interested in Dustin Peeler anymore. Now get out!"

I forgot she is no longer a Dustin Peeler fan. Emily changes her celebrity crushes so often, it's hard to keep up.

"Who do you like now?" I ask. "Maybe we could get him as a spokesperson or something."

"I like whoever picks you up and throws you out of my bedroom," she says, between blowing on her toenails to dry them. (Most people probably can't blow on their toenails, but Emily used to be a gymnast.)

I start to head out of her room. But when I reach the door, I turn back. "Did I mention you'll get paid?"

Emily looks up. "How much?"

I tell her the first hourly wage Manny told me to say. She tries to look unimpressed, but I see her eyebrows flicker. "I don't know," she drawls. "Seems awfully low."

I tell her the second hourly wage Manny told me to say. "Take it or leave it. I'm sure we can find someone else. It's just that we'd rather have a family member, since sometimes we talk about company secrets."

"Fine," she says. "I'll take it. But don't tell anyone. I don't want the word to get out that I'm spending my afternoons working for two geeks."

"That's not a very nice thing to call your boss," I can't help saying.

"Boss?" she says, making her stuffed sardine face again. "Yuck. Hey, what will you call me?"

"Um, Emily?" I say. "Maybe Ninja Spider, although I'm thinking you need a new nickname."

She looks at me like I'm an idiot. "No, I mean, like, what's my role going to be called at Sure Things, Inc.?"

Manny and I didn't discuss this. "I don't know . . . assistant?"

Emily looks even more disgusted. I wish

her face would freeze like that for a few days.

"Assistant in charge of Next Big Thing development?" I suggest, trying to make it sound more important.

She rolls her eyes. "If I'm going to do this, I want to be *vice president* in charge of . . . whatever you said."

"What do you mean *if* you do it? You already said you're doing it!"

"Am I vice president or not?"

I sigh. Manny isn't going to like this. "Fine. You can be vice president. But you still have to do what Manny and I tell you to do."

I dodge the pillow she throws at me.

Emily turns out to be much faster at going through the videos than Manny and I were. We felt like we had to watch the whole video, but Emily has no mercy. If the invention seems like a bad idea to her in the first few seconds, she goes on to the next video.

She uses her own system to classify the videos. She calls it the D.U.M.B. SYSTEM. Each video is given one of four labels:

D for Dumb (obviously),

U for Unoriginal,

M for Maybe (Manny and I watch all the *M*s), or

B for Brilliant. (So far Emily hasn't given a *B*.)

There are way more *D*s than anything else. She must be wearing out the *D* key on her laptop.

One afternoon a few days later Manny and I are in the office watching the videos Emily has tagged *M* for maybe. We've divided them between us to make the work go faster. If either of us finds an idea we think is decent, we share it with the other one.

We have earbuds in, so we can't hear each other's audio. But out of the corner of my eye I see Manny sit up straighter. He starts to smile. Then he takes his earbuds out and says, "I think you should watch this one."

I move over to his computer. He uses his mouse to click on the video's play button.

A girl appears on the screen. "Hello," she says in a very serious voice. "I believe my invention could be Sure Things' Next Big Thing. It is called the SIBLING SILENCER."

I like the sound of that.

The girl holds up something that looks like an oversized remote control. "The Sibling Silencer is a device designed to do exactly what it says: silence your sibling."

Now, there's an invention that could come in very, very handy.

"Unfortunately," the girl continues, "there are still a lot of bugs to work out. Allow me to demonstrate."

A boy walks into view. "This is my brother," the girl says, gesturing toward him. "Alan, please begin speaking."

"Hey," he says, "what are you doing? Can I play? What's that thing you've got? Can I try it? Mom says you have to let me play with you because I'm your little brother and you've got to be nice to me. If you don't I'm going to tell–"

Click! The girl presses a button on the remote control as she aims it at her brother.

"**Rowf! Rowf rowf arf arf arf! Meow! Meow! Moo moo moo moo! Oink! aRF!**" the boy says.

In the corner of the garage, Philo sits up and barks back. "**Woof!**"

"Thank you, Alan," the girl says. She gives him a cookie. Eating it, he steps out of the picture. "As you can see, or hear, the Sibling Silencer currently does not silence siblings. Instead, it reduces their speech to primitive animal sounds. With your help, I'm sure we can take sibling speech all the way down to silence. Thank you."

She takes a little bow, and the video ends.

"What do you think?" Manny asks.

"I liked it when the brother talked like a dog. And a cat. And a cow. And a pig. That was hilarious," I say. "But he could have been faking it. Maybe the remote control didn't really make him talk that way."

Manny nodded. "Yeah, I was thinking that too. We could ask the inventor to ship us the remote control, and we could test it out ourselves."

"True, if she's willing to ship her invention to us."

"She probably is. She trusts us enough to send us the video about her invention. But in a way, it really doesn't matter whether the brother's faking those animal noises or not."

I stand up and stretch. We've been looking at Emily's M videos for quite a while. "It doesn't?" I ask. "Why not?"

"Because we can handle the technology," Manny says. "The important thing is the idea. And I think the Sibling Silencer is a great idea."

"How do you know? You don't have any siblings."

"No," Manny admits. "But I've been around our new vice president enough to know that a Sibling Silencer would be pretty handy for you to have."

He's right. A Sibling Silencer would be pretty sweet. Just about anyone with sisters or brothers would want one. Manny starts hitting the keys on his computer.

"What are you doing?" I ask.

"E-mailing the inventor to tell her we're going to help her develop a working Sibling Silencer," he says.

"Wait! Slow down!" I yell. "Shouldn't we talk about this a little more?"

So we talk. But we still end up at the same conclusion: The Sibling Silencer should be Sure Things' Next Big Thing. I'm worried that I won't be able to figure out how to make it work, but Manny waves my worries aside. He's got all the confidence in the world in my inventing abilities.

Too bad I don't.

Because I know the truth about the All Ball.

Still, I can't think of a convincing reason to say no (other than the truth, and once again, I've chickened out on confessing), so Manny e-mails the girl who thought of the Sibling Silencer. Her name is Abby, and she's thrilled. She agrees to send us her prototype right away, along with detailed descriptions of all the work she's done so far.

Things are moving fast. Too fast.

We've got the prototype and Abby's plans, so I've been studying them. It was fun testing the prototype on Emily.

"WHAT ARE YOU DOING IN MY ROOM? GET OUT OF HERE OR I'LL TELL DAD THAT YOU'RE ARF ARF ARF ARF! MEOW! WOOF! MEOW! OINK!"

I've made some progress, but I'm still stumped by some details. And I'm really feeling the pressure. Manny's counting on me. Abby's counting on me. Sure Things, Inc. is counting on me. And siblings all over the world are counting on me, even if they don't know it yet.

A few days later Manny and I are working in the office. In the corner I've set up a minilab where I can run tests and do analyses. I'm trying out a few different approaches to certain details of the Sibling Silencer.

"How's it going?" Manny asks, coming over to the lab corner of the garage. He doesn't come to this part of the office all that often. He's usually too busy with his computer.

"Not great," I mumble, concentrating on a new wiring configuration.

"But it'll all come together soon, right? The Sibling Silencer?"

I shrug.

Manny holds up a printout of an e-mail. "Well," he says, "maybe this'll inspire you!"

"What is it?" I ask, taking the e-mail. I read it, and realize it's a letter from a producer of WAKE UP, AMERICA! saying they'd love to have us on their show to announce our Next Big Thing!

"There must be some mistake here," I say as I continue to read. "The date they're confirming is really soon!"

"That's no mistake," Manny says. "It's the perfect time to announce the new product."

"But we don't *have* a new product!" I say, trying not to shout. "We just have an idea. And I have no idea how long it will take me to turn the idea into something real that we can sell!"

Manny pats me on the shoulder. "You're the genius who invented the All Ball, remember? I figured scheduling this announcement on TV would motivate you!"

"I don't need motivation!" I say, much louder than I mean to. I try to speak in my normal voice. "That's a lot of pressure on me, Manny," I tell him.

"I have faith in you!" Manny replies, grinning at me. "Setting a deadline is one of the best ways to motivate a creative genius. I read that in one of my management journals."

Manny starts to walk away, but then he turns back. I'm pretty sure what he's about to say is the reason he came over to the lab in the first place.

"Actually," he says, looking at the floor, "we kind of *have* to have the Sibling Silencer soon."

"Why?" I ask.

Manny runs his fingers though his hair. "Because I kind of poured a lot of what we made on the All Ball into promoting the

Sibling Silencer. Without the Sibling Silencer, the whole company could go under."

"*Promoting* it? Already? But it doesn't exist!"

"You have to buy commercial time in advance," Manny explains. "And the holiday shopping season is crucial to the success of a new product like this. Every business journal says so," he adds before he walks away.

You need to steal Manny's business journals and file them away in the garbage can, I tell my hands.

I know Manny well enough to know he's not that worried. He really believes I can pull this off.

How do you tell your best friend that his best friend is a big fraud?

Chapter Eight

The Inventor Who Became a Zombie

NOW THAT I'VE GOT a DEADLINE, I'M SPENDING EVERY spare moment I can find working on the Sibling Silencer. I've got it to the point where it doesn't make siblings sound like animals, but they still speak gibberish.

This is what happened the last time I tested my prototype on Emily:

"YOU'D BETTER NOT BE POINTING THAT STUPID THING AT ME AGAIN, BECAUSE I'M GOING TO TELL GLARBLE FWIMBAH SCHNOOZAY KALAPP WHEEFEE!"

Funny, but not silent. Far from it. Emily

actually seemed to get a little louder after I zapped her with the remote control.

I've been working on the Sibling Silencer late into the night at my desk. My days are all the same: get up early to work on the Sibling Silencer, go to school, go to the office to work on the Sibling Silencer, come home to eat Dad's bad dinner (last night it was ragout of rutabaga), do my homework, work on the Sibling Silencer, and sleep. On the weekends I just leave out the school part. Oh, and walk Philo. I do that, too. But I've been making the walks shorter and shorter to save time.

And our appearance on **WAKE UP, AMERICA!** is getting closer and closer. . . .

At school one day I fall asleep at lunch. I end up facedown in my sloppy joe. Somebody takes a picture and posts it on the Internet with the caption "GENIUS AT WORK." Luckily, with my face in my lunch, you can't really tell if it's me or not. It could be anyone.

It's tough to stay awake in class, too. In science Mr. Palnacchio calls me up to the front to help him explain the Science of Color. I practically fall asleep leaning against the board and get red marker on my face. Jenny Starling raises her hand and asks, "Mr. Palnacchio, what's the science of getting color all over your face?" Everyone laughs.

I walk through the halls like a zombie. Dressing up like a zombie for Halloween is really fun, but actually feeling like a zombie? Not so much fun.

A sixth grader runs up to me. "Hey, Sure!"

I turn to him and mumble, "Yes?"

"I've got this great idea for an invention!" He lowers his voice so no one else can hear. "It's a pop-up changing room. You could use it on the beach, or even in the locker room so you wouldn't have to change right in front of everyone else."

Zombie Me automatically reaches into my pocket and pulls out my wallet.

I take one of Manny's Next Big Thing cards and hand it to the kid.

"What's this?" the kid asks, disappointed.

"Read it," I mutter. "Explains everything."

Then I zombie-walk my way down the hall toward my next class. Unless it features a unit on eating human brains, I'm probably not going to do very well.

But lack of sleep isn't my only problem. Every time I try to work on the Sibling Silencer, I hear this voice inside my head. It says things like this:

You're a fraud.

There's no way you can do this.

You're going to fail.

Your company will go bankrupt.

You'll go to prison.

Naturally, these thoughts don't exactly inspire me to do my best. But I keep on trying. Luckily, I really like the idea of the Sibling Silencer. Every day, Emily makes me like it even more.

Take now, for instance. I'm standing in the kitchen, minding my own business. (Okay, I'm standing here because I'm so tired I can't remember where I am supposed to be. But that's not the point.)

"What are you doing standing in the middle of the kitchen?" Emily demands. "Just standing there like a zombie? You are so *weird*. This town should build a weird museum and put you in it. You could be their main exhibit. If you're just going to stand there with your mouth hanging open, you give me no choice but to take your picture and post it on the Internet."

She pulls out her camera and takes my picture.

I stumble back up the stairs to my room. The plans for the Sibling Silencer are calling to me. And they have a really annoying voice that's not unlike Emily's annoying voice: "INVENT ME! COME ON, HURRY UP AND INVENT ME!"

Most nights, before I get too sleepy, I take a couple of minutes to write a quick e-mail to my mom. Somehow, just typing my troubles to her makes me feel a little better. It's nice to know that somewhere on the planet there's someone who loves you, even if you can't figure out how to invent a Sibling Silencer.

(I know my dad loves me, even if he does seem to be trying to punish me with his awful cooking. And I'm pretty sure Philo loves me no matter what.)

Hi, Mom,

Hope you're doing great, and that all your research is going well. We sure do miss you. Me especially. I don't actually know about Dad and Emily. I can't get inside their brains. (I don't think I'd want to get inside Emily's brain.) But I do know I miss you a lot.

School is fine. Lots of homework—lots more than in sixth grade, and I already thought that was kind of too much. But I'm keeping up with it, barely. (Don't worry, my grades are good.)

The All Ball's still really popular, and selling well. Manny says we expanded to five new countries this week. He calls them "new markets." To me, "market" seems like kind of a small word for a whole country.

Still working on the Next Big Thing. It's tricky. Hope I crack it soon, especially since we're already booked to announce it on a morning news show. That's Manny for you. Oh well. I owe him a lot.

The Hyenas are just about done with their season, unfortunately. There's always next year.

Love,
Billy

I hit send. Then I crawl into bed and fall fast asleep. The last thing I remember thinking is, *You're a fraud.*

• • •

The next day, I'm in the office, twirling the rods of the foosball game, knocking the ball back and forth from one end of the table to the other.

Klop! Klop! Klop! Klop!

I guess if Manny can play chess against himself, I can play foosball against myself. Except I'm not really playing. I'm thinking.

When he hears me knocking the ball back and forth, Manny looks up from his sales figures. "Wanna play a game?"

"No, thanks," I say. "I'm thinking."

"What about?"

"The Candy Brush. I had a thought about the flavor conversion unit. I'd like to test it out, but I'll need some new materials . . ."

Manny looked concerned. "That's great, Billy, but what about the Sibling Silencer? We've gotta go on that TV show and introduce it in just—"

"I KNOW!" I shout, surprising Manny and myself. Philo jumps to his feet to see what the matter is.

It's like a balloon of worry and guilt and stress has been getting bigger and bigger inside me until it finally popped. I take a deep breath. "I know," I say more quietly. "I haven't forgotten."

Manny gets up and comes over to the foosball table. "What's wrong? I know you're under a lot of pressure to come up with this Sibling Silencer, but you'll do it. Just like you did the All Ball."

It's time to tell him. I'm sick of this secret. Maybe I'm finally fed up, or maybe I'm just tired, but, either way, it's time to come clean to Manny.

"I didn't."

Manny looks totally confused. "Didn't what?"

"Didn't come up with the All Ball. I'm a complete fraud."

For a second Manny's speechless. "You mean you . . . *stole* the idea for the All Ball?

I shake my head. "No, I didn't steal it. It was . . . given to me."

"By who?"

"I don't know."

Manny sits down on the closest chair. "Okay, I'm totally confused. You didn't invent the All Ball, but you didn't steal it. Someone gave it to you. But you don't know who."

So I tell him everything. About how I was struggling with the plans for the All Ball, trying for the breakthrough that would make it possible. About how I went to bed, and in the morning the blueprints were right there on my desk in my bedroom. And how I was so excited to have the solution to the problem, I just shared it with Manny, forgetting to mention how I got it. And then the whole thing just took off like a rocket, and I was too busy (and guilty) to tell Manny where the plans came from.

I'm afraid Manny's going to be mad at me for holding out on him, but he isn't. He's just confused.

"That's . . . bizarre! Why would someone draw up blueprints and then just give them to you anonymously? And never come forward, even when the All Ball's a huge success? Who would do that?"

We talk about my family, since they were right there in the house. "Emily, no. Doesn't make sense," Manny says emphatically. "Your dad? He's a good artist. I bet he could draw plans."

"That's what I thought. But inventing's not his thing. Or keeping secrets."

"Your mom? Was she home then?"

"Yeah, she was home. I guess it's possible she did it. But I don't get why she wouldn't just say, 'Here. I did this for you.' She knows how guilty this secret would make me feel, and she wouldn't want to do that."

"Guilty?" Manny says, making a face. "Listen, whoever left those blueprints for you *wanted* you to use them! They *wanted* you to make the All Ball! And you did. So you did exactly what they wanted you to do! You have nothing to feel guilty about."

Somehow I'd never thought about it that way. I feel about ten thousand times better. Reason #1001 why Manny is the greatest CFO and best friend: He always makes me feel better when I'm superlow.

"How about a slice?" Manny suggests. We go to the pizza dispenser and pick our toppings.

"Okay," Manny says after he's bitten through a long string of mozzarella cheese, "now I understand why you've been feeling like a fraud. But let me ask you something. Before these mysterious blueprints showed up, had you done some work on the All Ball?"

I chew and swallow. "Yeah, of course. You know I had. Tons of work. I'd been working for weeks."

"And were the blueprints completely different from anything you'd come up with?"

"No. They followed the same lines I'd been following. But they solved a couple of crucial problems that had stumped me."

Manny smiled. "That's what I thought. See, you're not a fraud at all. You're still an inventor. I've known you a long time, and I think you're a genius."

That's really nice to hear. I don't think Manny's ever actually called me that. Emily's called me genius lots of times, but she's always being sarcastic. I can tell that Manny really means it.

Manny finishes his slice. He picks up a small All Ball and starts tossing it up toward the ceiling and catching it. "So it seems to me that you've just lost your confidence. The mystery of where these blueprints came from is eating you up inside."

I pick up the All Ball's remote and aim it at the ball. When it goes up, it's a golf ball. When it comes down, it's a tennis ball. Manny catches it and tosses it like he doesn't even notice the change.

"What we have to do," Manny continues, "is solve that mystery, so you can stop thinking about it and concentrate on the Sibling Silencer."

The ball goes up a tennis ball and comes down a hockey puck.

"How are we going to solve it?" I ask.

"I don't know," Manny admits. "But figuring out a way to solve the blueprint mystery is my new number-one priority. Right now, that is the most important thing!"

The ball goes up a hockey puck and comes down a Ping-Pong ball.

"More important than sales figures?" I ask with a small smile.

Manny's so shocked by that idea he drops the Ping-Pong ball. It bounces across the garage floor and Philo chases it.

"Let's not get crazy!" Manny says.

Chapter Nine

Manny with a Plan

THAT NIGHT I SLEEP BETTER THAN I HAVE IN WEEKS.

At breakfast Emily says, "Not that I really want to, but do you need me to look at more of those stupid videos? I could use the money."

"For what? Did they get a new shipment of clothes at Goths 'R' Us?" I ask as I eat my bowl of cereal. (Luckily, Dad hasn't turned his gourmet ambitions to breakfast. Yet. He likes to paint early in the morning. He says he loves the light.)

"Ha-ha," Emily says. "Hilarious, genius. So do you need your vice president again or what?"

"Not right now," I answer. "We've got more on our plate than we can handle. The last thing we need is another Next Big Thing. But I guess eventually we'll have to get back to the videos. They keep coming in."

She looks disappointed for a second, but her face quickly slides back into *who cares* mode. "Okay, whatever," she says, getting up from the table. "There's always asking Dad for money. I think I'll ask him right now. Here's a little tip from your big sister: When he's painting, Dad'll say yes to just about anything so he can get right back to his work."

Like I don't already know that. How does she think I got permission to get Philo in the first place?

My school day really isn't that bad. Having gotten some decent sleep really helps make the day better! Plus, no one asks me to lend them money, or teach their class, or give an inspirational speech. I hand out a couple of Next Big Thing cards, but by now most of the kids at Fillmore Middle School who have ideas for inventions have already gotten cards.

One of the kids I give a card to is a short sixth grader. His invention idea is "underpants that secretly make you strong, like a superhero." Since I'm not feeling like a zombie today, I actually smile and encourage him to keep working on it.

"Make a video and send it in!" I say.

"I will!" he says, taking the card and running off. When he gets to the end of the hall, he sticks his arms out like he's flying.

When I stop back home before going to the office, I pick up Philo. As usual he's thrilled to see me.

Philo seems to be in a rush to get to the office. Maybe he's hoping for some pizza. He's really pulling on the leash, so we start running. Philo practically drags me all the way to Manny's house.

"Hey!" I say as I enter the office. "How's it going? How are the latest sales figures?"

"Oh, I haven't checked," Manny says.

That's unusual.

"I've been too busy thinking about your problem, the blueprint mystery. And I think I've come up with a way to solve it!"

I take off Philo's leash and hang it on a hook. He does a quick sniff-around and then settles into his bed in the corner. I toss him a treat from a jar we keep at the office.

"Great!" I tell Manny.

Manny dispenses himself an orange-lime cola and takes a drink. Then he says, "Okay, here's what I'm thinking."

He walks over to a dry-erase board mounted to the garage door. He sets his drink on a table and picks up a marker.

"Some nice person left you the blueprints for the All Ball," he says, drawing a smiling face on the whiteboard. "Let's call them X." He writes a big X above the face.

"Hi, X," I say.

Manny continues. "Person X obviously wanted to help you. He or she likes you. Maybe even loves you." He draws a heart on the board.

"So I'm guessing that if this person sees you

really worried about another invention, they'll want to help you again," Manny says, drawing a worried face, with a frowning mouth and eyebrows pointing up. "That's just logical."

"Another invention? You mean like the Sibling Silencer?"

"Exactly!" Manny says, writing *Sib Sil* on the board. "Have you been talking to your family about your struggles?"

I think about it and shake my head. "No," I say. "I guess Dad and Emily might have noticed me working late in my room, but I haven't said anything about what I'm working on. I don't want Dad to worry. Emily probably knows we picked the Sibling Silencer, since I've tested it on her a couple of times, but I doubt she knows I'm worried about it. Or cares."

Manny smiles. "I think it's time to lay out the bait and let them know you're worried."

Manny, Philo, and I walk into the house just in time for dinner. "What's that smell?" Manny whispers, looking scared.

Dad's in the kitchen, cooking.

"Don't worry," I reassure Manny. "It'll be okay. Remember, you're doing this for the good of Sure Things, Inc. The company's very existence may depend on your ability to eat my dad's cooking."

Manny still looks scared. "But I don't know if I can."

"If it gets really bad," I whisper, "just suck on the ice cubes in your drink before you take a bite. The cold helps kill the taste."

"Can't I just sneak my food to Philo?" Manny asks. "I thought that's what dogs were for. They're like garbage disposals with legs."

I shake my head. "When Dad's cooking, Philo steers clear of the kitchen."

Manny sniffs the air. "Smart dog."

"Hey, Dad," I say as we walk into the kitchen. "Is it okay if Manny stays for dinner?"

Dad looks up from chopping something that resembles a brain. "Of course! We've got plenty! Manny, you can tell me what you think of my latest creation."

"What are you making?" Manny asks, trying to erase all the fear from his voice.

"MAC AND CHEESE!" says Dad.

Manny breathes a sigh of relief.

"With garlic and cauliflower!" Dad continues.

"Wow, my two favorites," Manny says. "I always ask for them on my birthday instead of cake."

"Well, isn't that lucky!" Dad cries, not picking up on Manny's sarcasm. "I'll have to give you an EXTRA-BIG PORTION!"

The blood drains from Manny's face.

Since Manny's here, we eat in the dining room instead of the breakfast nook. Dad even gets out our nicer plates and the real glasses instead of the plastic ones.

"Are we celebrating something?" Emily asks, puzzled.

"Sure, why not?" Dad says. "Let's celebrate the success of the All Ball and Sure Things, Inc.! We've all been so busy that we haven't really taken the time to celebrate together!"

As we push the food around on our plates,

holding ice cubes in our mouths, Manny and I exchange a look. Dad's just given us a good cue to put our plan into action.

"Thanks, Dad," I say, trying a bite of the mutant mac and cheese and then quickly spitting it into my napkin. "But actually, to tell the truth, things aren't going all that smoothly at Sure Things, Inc."

Dad stops eating to look at me, concerned. "Really? What's the matter? Is one of the big sports equipment companies giving you trouble? They're probably not too happy having five of their products replaced by just one of yours. But that's business! COMPETITIVE!"

As an artist, Dad basically knows one thing about business: It's competitive. He says that's why he never wanted to go into business, but from what I've seen, art is incredibly competitive too. Maybe even more than business.

"No," I say, "it's not that. It's the new product we're working on. Our Next Big Thing."

"I helped them find it," Emily volunteers in a smug voice. "I'm their D.U.M.B. vice president."

Dad gives Emily a look. He doesn't know that Emily uses the D.U.M.B. system. "That's not a very nice thing to call yourself."

Manny says the stuff we decided he'd say. (He actually insisted on writing it down and memorizing it.) "You see, Mr. Sure—"

"Please, Manny," Dad interrupts. "Call me Bryan."

"Okay . . . Bryan," Manny says a little awkwardly. "Anyway, developing a new product is very challenging. Billy's got to solve a lot of problems and get everything just right. And unfortunately, I've put some extra pressure on him."

We explain about the deadline for the Sibling Silencer and how we have to have it ready in time to demonstrate it on the national morning news show.

"I don't care when you have to have it ready," Emily says. "You're not testing it on me again!" She turns to Dad. "Billy tested it on me, Dad. Like I was some kind of . . . lab rat or something."

"Billy, stop using your sister as a lab rat,"

Dad says to me automatically. "So you're worried about inventing this Sibling Silencer thing in time? Meeting your deadline?"

I nod a little too vigorously. "Exactly. So worried. SO VERY WORRIED. SO VERY, VERY WORRIED."

Emily shoots me a look. "And so very, very weird."

I ignore her. "In fact, I'm so worried that I don't think I'll be able to finish my dinner."

Dad looks a little crestfallen. "Oh dear." Then he perks up. "Still, that just means more for you, Manny!" He ladles another big helping onto Manny's plate.

• • •

After dinner Manny comes up to my room.

"How do you think it went?" I ask.

"Eating that dinner made me never want to eat again," Manny groans, clutching his stomach.

"I don't mean the food," I say. "I mean our plan. Do you think they got the message? That I'm worried about inventing the Sibling Silencer?"

Manny nods, smiling a little. "I think so. I think they picked up your subtle hint: 'I'm so worried. So very, very worried.'"

I hold up my hands. "Okay, so I may have overdone it a little bit."

"Or a lot."

"The important thing is, now my dad and Emily both know I'm worried. So if either one of them slipped me the blueprints for the All Ball, they might do it again for the Sibling Silencer."

"What about your mom? Should you send her a worried e-mail?"

I'd been thinking about that. "No, because she's on the other side of the planet, probably, so even if she wanted to help me out, she couldn't just fly home and sneak some blueprints onto my desk. So now what?"

Manny jumps up enthusiastically and walks over to my dry-erase board. He picks up a blue marker. "Okay!" he says. "We've laid out the bait. Now we just have to set the trap!"

For good measure, he writes TRAP on the whiteboard.

"What are we trying to catch, exactly?" I ask. All this talk of bait and traps has got me a little confused.

"For a genius, you can be kind of an idiot," Manny says in a friendly voice. "We're trying to catch whoever put the All Ball blueprints on your desk. Let's call him or her the antithief." He tries to draw a rolled-up set of blueprints on the board, but they end up kind of looking like a burrito. Which I could go for right about now.

"Are we thinking some kind of cage that drops down from the ceiling?" I ask.

Manny thinks for a minute, tapping on the whiteboard with his marker, leaving little blue marks. "As much as I like the idea of a cage, I

122

think it presents several problems. One: How would we hang it in your room so that the antithief wouldn't notice?"

"Unless it was an invisible cage, like a force field of some kind," I suggest.

"We seem to keep coming back to force fields, but we have to admit they don't actually exist yet," Manny points out.

"True. And we don't have time to invent one."

"Right. Let's put force fields on hold for now," Manny agrees. "So when we say 'trap,' we don't necessarily mean a cage. We might just mean some kind of alarm that goes off, waking you so you catch the antithief red-handed."

To indicate the alarm, Manny draws a bell on the board.

"An alarm sounds good to me," I say, getting up and walking over to pet Philo.

"It'd be pretty simple to rig up alarms that get tripped by someone knocking into or stepping on something," I go on. "Like a booby trap. If someone is trying to leave blueprints for the Sibling Silencer on my desk and unknowingly

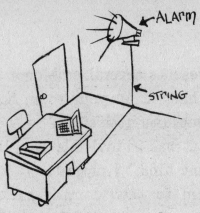

ALARM

STRING

steps on a piece of string, an alarm goes off."

I draw a simple diagram on the dry-erase board. "We'll attach one end of a piece of string to my desk and the other end to an alarm, but make sure it's low enough so that the antithief doesn't trip on the string. But tight enough so if you step on the string, you trip the alarm. We can plant a few of these so that the antithief is sure to step on one."

It doesn't take us long to put together an alarm system with stuff I have in my bedroom.

"There," I say, stepping back to admire our work. "If someone tries to put another set of plans on my desk in the middle of the night, I'll know it right away."

"Let's hope they do," Manny says, crossing his fingers. "We really need those plans."

Chapter Ten

an antithief in the Night

I STAY UP LATE, WORKING ON THE SIBLING SILENCER.
I want everything to seem normal, so the antithief won't suspect anything.

Finally, I go to bed. I'm thinking so much about the antithief and the alarm system that I can't concentrate on the Sibling Silencer anyway. Philo's already been asleep in his doggy bed for a couple of hours. He seems to be dreaming, because he twitches and makes little snuffling and yipping sounds in his sleep.

I lie in the dark. The house is quiet. I think about the Sibling Silencer and the last couple of snags I've hit. Then my eyes start to droop. They close. I'm breathing more slowly . . .

Brrree-doop! Brrree-doop! Brrree-doop!

The alarm! It's going off! My lights have snapped on!

I see my clock. It's the middle of the night. I must have fallen asleep.

Still groggy, I look around for the anti-thief. But the only other living being in the room is Philo. He's sitting in the middle of the room, staring at me. He lifts a paw, hoping for a treat.

I use a remote control to shut off the alarm. When I set the alarm's volume, I made sure it was loud enough to wake me up, but not so loud that it'd wake up anyone else in the house. I listen for footsteps, but hear nothing except the ticking of a clock downstairs.

I decide to check my desk.

There's something on it!

I can't believe it. Another set of blueprints! When I examine them, it's clear that they're the plans to build a Sibling Silencer.

SIBLING SILENCER

And they look perfect. Brilliant, in fact. The stumbling blocks that I just couldn't get over have been pushed aside. Everything's solved. With these plans, there's nothing standing between me and a working Sibling Silencer. I'm basically holding Sure Things' Next Big Thing in my hands. I can't believe it.

So it's happened again. But we didn't catch anyone!

I spend a few more minutes studying the blueprints, then I put them in a drawer and lock it. I turn off the lights.

Back in bed my mind races. How could someone have come into my room, put blueprints on the desk, tripped the alarm, and then disappeared before I saw them? I'm sure I woke up as soon as the alarm went off.

Philo stands up and scratches his bed, as though he's trying to make it softer, like someone plumping a pillow. He does this every night, even though his bed never gets any softer. He's only managed to rip out the bottom of the bed.

He was the only one in my bedroom when the alarm went off. But a dog couldn't possibly have been the one to figure out the blueprints.

Could he?

I wake up the next morning after a night full of dreams about Philo doing amazingly smart things: going to college, becoming a professor, winning a Nobel Prize made out of bacon.

It's early, and Philo is still sleeping, curled up in his dog bed. He just looks like a normal dog. And that's all he is, right?

I think about when we first got him. I had been begging for a dog for months, and finally Dad said yes one morning when he was painting. We went to the shelter, and Philo stuck his paw out of the cage when I walked by. Like he was choosing me.

It's a Saturday, so I don't have to go to school today. I have all day to solve the mystery of how the blueprints appeared on my desk.

Philo wakes up. He stands, stretches, and looks at me, ready to go outside for his morning bathroom break.

I look at him. In the light of day, I realize that it was pretty ridiculous to wonder if he could have written the blueprints. He almost definitely didn't do it. But maybe he can tell me who did. When I look into Philo's eyes, it sometimes seems like he's thinking. Like he's got something he wants to tell me.

Usually it's *I would like a treat, please.*

But maybe he has more to say today. Secrets that want to spill out of that little doggie brain. And if I'm clever enough, maybe I can figure out a way to communicate with him.

"Woof!" Philo says, impatient to go outside. At least, I *think* that's what he's saying. If only I had a DOG TRANSLATOR.

Now that's a great idea! Maybe that should be our *next* Next Big Thing, after the Sibling Silencer, of course.

"Come on, Philo," I say. "Let's go outside." The second I say "go," Philo gets excited. We head downstairs. I grab Philo's leash, clip it to his collar, and head out the back door.

He accomplishes his goal.

But we stay out in the yard. The gate's closed, so I unclip his leash and let him wander around, sniffing the ground.

I pull out my phone and start searching for information about dog intelligence. I read that dogs can understand up to TWO HUNDRED WORDS!

If Philo can understand two hundred human words, then that means he can understand two hundred ideas. And if he can understand two hundred ideas, it seems like one of those ideas could be, *I know who left those blueprints on your desk last night.* If only he could *say* two hundred words.

As we go back inside the house, we run into Dad, headed out to the little art studio he built in our backyard. "Good morning!" he says. As he scratches behind Philo's ears, I want to ask Philo, *Was it him? Did he do it? You can tell me!*

Maybe I can get Dad to admit to it. "How was your night?" I ask innocently.

"What do you mean?" he asks, puzzled. We're both pretty sure this is the first time in my life I've ever asked him how his night was.

"How'd you sleep?"

"Great! Like a rock, all night long! How 'bout you?"

I think about telling him what happened. But not just yet. I'm still trying to figure it all out. If he did leave the blueprints, he's doing an awfully good job of pretending he didn't. And Dad's not much of an actor. When it comes to keeping secrets, my dad is the worst. You can tell he's hiding one because every time he looks at you, his eyes get wide and he purses his lips like he's trying not to say something. It makes him look like a fish.

"I slept okay," I say, checking his face for anything fishy.

"That's good!" he says. "I know you're worried about your next invention, so I'm glad you could sleep. Sleep's important. It's tough to be creative when you're short on sleep."

"How do you know I'm worried about my next invention?" I ask suspiciously.

"Because you said so—repeatedly—at dinner last night!" Dad laughs.

Oh, right.

Philo and I go inside. I feed him and get myself a bowl of cereal and add some blueberries on top. While I'm in the kitchen, Emily stumbles in, rubbing her eyes.

"Why is everyone so loud?" she complains. "It's Saturday. I wanted to sleep in! But you and Philo and Dad are so loud. Ugh."

She opens the refrigerator and stares.

"Sorry," I say. "Did you, um, have trouble sleeping last night?"

"What?" she asks, still staring at the contents of the fridge as though she hopes something delicious will materialize right in front of her eyes.

"Were you awake in the night? Did you get up? Or see anything?"

She finally turns her head and looks at me as if I've lost my mind. "What are you talking about? Did *you* see something?" She closes the fridge without taking anything out. "You didn't see a ghost, did you? I always thought this house was haunted. Remember that time I woke up and there were strange orbs on my walls?"

I remember that night. I don't tell her that I was playing a prank on her with a mirror and a flashlight.

"No, and I don't believe in ghosts," I say.

"You would if you saw one," she insists.

This talk of ghosts is getting us nowhere. I change the subject. "Hey, Em, do you think dogs are smart?"

She opens a cabinet and stares at the boxes of cereal. "As opposed to what?" she asks. "You? Yes, I think dogs are brilliant."

"You think Philo is smart?"

She looks at Philo, walks over to him, leans down, and rubs the sides of his face. "Nope! He's just a big dumb pup!" Philo licks her face. "Kisses!" she squeals. "Kisses!"

"You know, they say dogs can understand up to two hundred words. I wish Philo could tell us what he knows. And what he sees, like, in the night."

I watch her carefully to see if she looks suspicious or guilty because I'm getting too close to her secret. She doesn't. She just looks as though she thinks I'm crazy. I've seen that look many, many times.

I finish my cereal, put the bowl in the dishwasher, and whistle to Philo. "Come on, boy! Come on!" He follows me up to my room. I've got an idea. I want to try something.

I close the bedroom door behind us. I'm used to Emily calling me insane, but there's no need to give her more reason to think so.

After finding the key and unlocking the drawer, I take out the Sibling Silencer blueprints. "Sit!" I say to Philo. He sits. "Sit" is definitely one of the words he knows.

Kneeling down, I show Philo the Sibling Silencer blueprints. "Remember these, boy? From last night?"

Philo licks the blueprints. But just once. Apparently they don't taste all that great.

"Did you see who brought these into my room last night and put them on my desk? Bark once for yes, twice for no."

Philo just sits there, looking like he's grinning, with his tongue flapping out of his mouth.

I look on my bookshelves and find a framed picture of me and my dad. I point to him. "Was it him? Did he bring the blueprints? Bark once for yes and twice for no."

Nothing.

I search through my junkiest drawer in the closet. I must have a picture of Emily somewhere. Oh, wait! My phone! Duh! I slide through the pictures on my phone and find a good one of Emily looking mad, telling me to get out of her room. I show it to Philo.

"Did Emily bring the blueprints? Bark once for yes, twice for no."

Philo licks the phone's screen.

I find a framed picture of my mother. "Was it Mom? Bark once for yes and twice for—"

"Woof!"

He barked! Once! Could it be? Could my mom have somehow found out I was worried, come home, slipped into my room, left the blueprints, and slipped back out before I woke up?

Twick twick twock-a twang twang biddly bong!

My phone's ringing! Is it Mom?

But it's only Manny.

"Billy!" he shouts when I answer. "Meet me at the office right away. I've got to show you something! Bye!"

"Wait!" I say. "Last night the alarm went off! I've got the blueprints for the Sibling Silencer!"

"I know! And I know who the antithief is!"

Chapter Eleven

The antithief, Revealed

AS I RACE OVER TO THE OFFICE ON MY BIKE, MY MIND'S spinning even faster than my wheels. Who gave me the blueprints? Mom? Dad? Emily? Philo? A ghost?

Or does Manny know who did it because he did it *himself*?

I've got the Sibling Silencer blueprints in my backpack, which bounces against my back as I pedal as hard as I can. I arrive at the office and wheel my bike right in through the side door we use as our only entrance and exit. I immediately ask, "Who did it?"

Manny doesn't even look up from his laptop. "Who did what?"

I guess he thinks this is funny. I feel like whacking him over the head with the blueprints until he spills the beans. I hold myself back.

"You know what! Who put the blueprints for the Sibling Silencer on my desk last night, and set off the alarm, and then mysteriously disappeared?"

Manny spins around in his desk chair and pretends he just now remembers what I'm talking about. "Oh, that! Right! Would you like to meet the person who did all that?"

I look around the office wildly. Is my mom here? Or someone else? I don't see anybody, and there aren't really any good hiding places in the office. I guess you could crouch under the pinball machine, but you'd still be easy to spot. And I'm not spotting anyone.

"Yeah," I say, walking quickly over to him. "I would very much like to meet him. Or her. Or it, if it's some kind of robot alien mutant

ROBOT ALIEN MUTANT Creature

creature. Just tell me who left the blueprints in my room!"

Manny smiles. "You did."

I just stand there for a few seconds, stunned. "W-what?" I manage to stammer.

"You did it," Manny repeats. "You drew up the Sibling Silencer blueprints and left them on your desk. You drew up the All Ball blueprints too."

"Manny, last night I went to sleep and there were no blueprints. I woke up and there were blueprints. How could it possibly have been me?"

"Here," he says, turning back to his computer. "I'll show you."

He clicks on a video.

"Hey, that's my room!" I say.

It's dark. There's kind of an eerie green glow, but I can make out my desk. Then a figure slowly moves into the shot.

It's me.

As I watch in complete amazement, I see myself sit at my desk, busily writing on blueprint paper.

"I'm using my left hand," I say.

"I know," Manny says. "It seems that when you're awake, you're right-handed. But when you're asleep, you're left-handed. As far as superpowers go, it's not the most exciting."

The video goes on for quite a while with me sitting at my desk, writing blueprints.

"I'm going to fast-forward to the important part," Manny says. He does, and in the video I make little jerky movements as I write in fast motion. Then he puts it back on regular speed. "Watch. Here it comes."

In the video I finish writing. I stand up and walk back to my bed.

"I never tripped the alarm."

"Because you knew where the strings were.

After all, you're the one who set up the trap."

I watch myself get in bed. Philo wakes up. He stands and walks around the room. He passes by my desk. The alarm goes off! The lights snap on!

By the time I sit up in bed, Philo's just sitting in the middle of the room.

Manny shuts off the video.

"I don't get it," I say. "I sleepwalk? And I . . . sleep-invent? Is that even a thing?"

"Apparently it is," Manny says, nodding. "And you do a really good job of it too."

"But where did this video come from?"

"I set up a webcam with night vision in your room and streamed the video to my computer."

"When?"

"When you were setting up the alarm yesterday. You were concentrating so hard, you didn't even notice."

I guess sometimes I really *can* focus. "But why did you do it?"

Manny took a deep breath and let it out. "Well, I've known for a long time that you walk and talk in your sleep. After six years of sleepovers, you tend to pick up on details like that."

"Okay, so I sleepwalk sometimes. But sleep-invent?"

"I was sure you invented the All Ball by yourself. And I knew you were going to crack the Sibling Silencer. But I knew you wouldn't believe it unless I had proof."

The truth starts to sink in. And it feels good. I really did invent the All Ball! By myself! And now I've invented the Sibling Silencer! With Abby!

"Hey, we've got to tell Abby that I cracked the Sibling Silencer! Let's call her right now. We, uh, don't have to mention the part about the sleep-inventing."

Manny grins. "All right. But first let me see those blueprints. I want to admire your latest sleep-work."

Abby's thrilled when she hears that I've figured out how to make the Sibling Silencer work.

(We don't tell her I finished it in my sleep. Some things are trade secrets.) On the phone, she screams, "MY INVENTION! IT'S GOING TO BE A REAL THING!" In the background we hear her brother Alan say, "And I'm going to use it on you!" I can't help but think that parents are also going to love the Sibling Silencer, because bickering kids will end up silencing each other. And Manny loves it because no family will be able to buy just one!

Now that I have the completed blueprints, I get right to work making a prototype. Once I've ordered a few special parts and they've arrived, I'm able to put the Sibling Silencer together quickly, working in the office and the minilab in my bedroom.

As soon as I finish the prototype, I burst into Emily's room, hiding the Sibling Silencer behind my back. "WHAT ARE YOU DOING IN HERE?" she yells. "DIDN'T YOU EVER HEAR OF KNOCKING? YOU CAN'T JUST BARGE INTO MY ROOM WHENEVER YOU FEEL LIKE IT! I'M TELLING DAD!"

I whip the Sibling Silencer out and take aim . . .

"DON'T YOU POINT THAT THING AT ME! I TOLD YOU NOT TO—"

Shhhhhhoop!

Emily's mouth keeps moving, but no sound comes out. EUREKA! IT WORKS!

The device silences her beautifully, but of course it doesn't stop her from jumping up off her bed and running straight at me, giving me a murderous look while still moving her mouth.

I turn and run out of the house.

In a few seconds Emily's able to talk again. Even though I've run all the way down the street, I can still hear her screaming. "I AM

NOT YOUR GUINEA PIG FOR YOUR STUPID EXPERIMENTS! I AM YOUR VICE PRESIDENT! YOU ARE NOT ALLOWED TO EXPERIMENT ON YOUR VICE PRESIDENT!"

Once Emily cools down, I make my way back to our house and cut around through the side yard to Dad's art studio in the back. "Dad?" I ask as I open the door and peek in. "Sorry to interrupt . . ."

"That's okay, Billy! Come on in! I'm done for the day. Just washing my brushes."

He's dunking paintbrushes in various jars of liquid and shaking them.

"I wonder if you'd mind helping me test our latest invention."

"Not at all! What do you need me to do?"

"Just talk."

"What about?"

"Anything. How about . . . cleaning your paintbrushes?"

"You got it. Well, here I have a jar full of turpentine. So I take one of the brushes I used today and . . ."

I aim and hit the button. **Shhhhhhoop!**

". . . if that doesn't work, then I take this stiff metal brush, and I—"

"Thanks, Dad!"

"That's it?"

"That's it!"

I had to make sure that the Sibling Silencer only silenced siblings. It didn't silence Dad, so that was a very good sign. He's a family member, but obviously he's not my sibling.

I keep testing and refining the Sibling Silencer, trying to make it perfect. Manny finds a great manufacturer, and they assure us that we'll have a whole box of the products ready just in time for our appearance on WAKE UP. AMERICA!

My dad even does some artwork for us to use on the boxes and in the ads. His pictures feature happy boys and girls using the Sibling Silencer to silence their noisy sisters and brothers.

Finally, it's time to introduce the Sibling Silencer on WAKE UP. AMERICA! I fly back to

New York, but this time I don't feel so nervous.

Soon I'm standing backstage with another assistant's hand on my shoulder. I hear, "Let's meet Billy Sure, the twelve-year-old inventor of the All Ball!" The assistant gives me a gentle shove, and I walk out onto the set.

It's bright, just like the **Better Than Sleeping!** set. But this time there are two hosts. Bob Roberts and Cassidy Tyson.

After we talk a little about the All Ball, Bob says, "So, Billy, I understand you've got a new invention that you'd like to show us."

"That's right," I say, reaching behind the couch to where I know they've put a few boxes of our new product. "It's called the Sibling Silencer." I pull out a box and show it to them. Dad's artwork looks great. I explain about Sure Things' Next Big Thing contest, the Sibling Silencer, and how Abby came up with the idea and then I helped figure it out.

Bob and Cassidy laugh. "Does the Sibling Silencer do what I think it does?" Cassidy asks.

"Would you like a demonstration?" I ask.

"Absolutely!" she says.

"Emily? Would you come out here, please?"

Emily comes onstage. I realize that she's changed into a blue dress. I guess her all-black phase is over. I wonder what's going to come next. She smiles and gives the camera a little wave.

I stand up and gesture toward Emily. "This is my sister, Emily."

"Nice to meet you, Emily," says Cassidy. "Welcome!"

"Emily," I ask (though we've planned and rehearsed all this ahead of time), "would you yell at me a little, please?"

"Certainly," Emily says politely. I'm not sure, but it almost sounds like she says it in a British accent. Strange. But then again, Emily is strange. She clears her throat, takes a deep breath, and starts doing what she does best, although definitely in a British accent. "BILLY! DID YOU GO INTO MY ROOM TODAY? BECAUSE IF YOU SET ONE STINKING FOOT IN MY ROOM, I'M GOING TO—"

Shhhhhhoop!

Emily's mouth keeps moving, but no sound comes out of it. Not a peep.

"Very impressive!" says Cassidy, laughing and applauding. "I have three older brothers, so I really could have used one of these when I was a kid. As a matter of fact, I could *still* use one!"

"Wait a minute," Bob says. "I don't mean to sound suspicious, but how do we know Emily's not just *pretending* to be unable to speak?"

"I thought you might say that," I say. I call offstage, "Tony, would you come out here, please?"

A man just a little older than Bob walks out smiling. Bob looks completely surprised. "Tony! It's my brother, Tony, everyone! What a wonderful surprise!" He gets up and hugs his brother.

I hand a Sibling Silencer to Tony. Then I ask Bob to start talking. "No problem there. That's what he does best," Cassidy jokes.

"Well, I'm not sure what to say," Bob begins.

"I guess I could tell you about the time Tony's pants ripped right down the middle of his—"

Shhhhhhoop!

Bob goes silent! He keeps trying to speak, but no sound comes out of his mouth.

"Well, *here's* a first!" says Cassidy. "This is the longest I think he's ever gone without talking!"

In a few seconds, Bob's voice returns. "That was unbelievable!" he says.

"How did it feel?" Cassidy asks. "Did it hurt?"

"Not at all," he answers. "I just couldn't make any sound. It was the weirdest thing!" He picks up one of the boxes. "I've got to get one of these things! Payback time, Tony."

"Me too!" says Cassidy. She looks straight into the camera. "Watch out, big brothers! I'm comin' for ya!"

Chapter Twelve

Success!

IN THE OFFICE THE NEXT DAY MANNY AND I RAISE TWO glasses of soda. Mine's black-cherry ginger ale and his is a white-chocolate grape-orange float.

"To the Sibling Silencer!" I toast.

"And its unbelievable sales figures!" Manny adds. "Thanks to Abby and you and your genius inventing ability."

I sip my soda. "But also huge thanks to you, Manny. Not just for your business wizardry, but for showing me that I really did figure out the All Ball and the Sibling Silencer."

"I guess from now on whenever you get

stuck on a new invention, you should just go to bed!"

We laugh. I toss a large All Ball in the air. When it reaches the height of my toss, Manny zaps it with the remote control, changing it before it falls. It goes from football to basketball.

"Be careful not to hit the bowling ball button," I say.

"You know," Manny says, "there was someone who knew all along that you invented the All Ball and the Sibling Silencer in your sleep."

"Who?"

"Philo! He saw the whole thing! Both times!"

"That's true. If only he could have told me, I would've been spared an awful lot of guilt." I set down the All Ball and go over to pet

Philo. "I'm thinking we've got to invent a Dog Translator. Every dog owner in the world will want one!"

Just before I go to bed that night, I check my e-mail one more time. There's one from my mom. But I notice it's from her old e-mail address. Did she switch back to the one that got hacked? Why would she do that?

I click on the e-mail.

Hi, Honey!
   I am *so* sorry you haven't heard anything from me for a few weeks.

Huh? I just had an e-mail from her a couple of days ago. What's she talking about? Is this an old e-mail that just now came through for some reason?

I keep reading. . . .

I've been in Antarctica, and terrible storms knocked out the Wi-Fi at the station, so I haven't been able to e-mail you. I feel just terrible about it. I've been thinking about you, wondering how seventh grade is going. Of course, I've also missed the end of the Hyenas' season! I assume they didn't make the play-offs again this year . . .

The e-mail goes on, but I stop reading.

So my mom hasn't had e-mail for weeks.

Which raises a number of very important questions.

Who have I been e-mailing?

Who have I been telling my ideas for inventions?

Who has been pretending to be my mom?

And why?

BILLY SURE
·KID ENTREPRENEUR·
AND THE STINK SPECTACULAR

INVENTED BY LUKE SHARPE
DRAWINGS BY GRAHAM ROSS

I've got to talk to Manny. Even if it ruins his good mood. And even if what I've done could destroy our business forever. I've still got to tell him. We'll figure this out together. That's what best friends—and business partners—are for.

I get up and go to the bathroom. I'm ready to head downstairs to pour myself a bowl of cereal. Philo trots down the stairs ahead of me. It's Saturday, so I don't have to rush to school. But now that I've decided to tell Manny about Imposter Mom, I can't wait to get it over with. But my stomach is growling, so I need to eat first.

But then I smell something that makes me lose my appetite. Something . . . awful. I freeze.

Emily comes out of her bedroom. "Eww. What is that foul *smell*? Is it you, genius?"

Emily often calls me genius. But when she says it, it's not a compliment.

And she says it all with a British accent. But she's not British. Despite that little fact, she's been speaking with a British accent for the past few days. I have no idea why. But I have learned from experience with Emily that sometimes it's best not to ask why.

"It's not me," I say, heading downstairs again. "Maybe it's your accent. That stinks pretty bad."

"Wait!" she says. "Stop!"

I stop. I have no idea why she's telling me to stop. Is there a rattlesnake on the stairs? Nah, I think Philo would have noticed.

"I know what the horrid odor is," she says dramatically.

"What?"

"Dad's cooking breakfast!"

If she's right, this is a terrible development. My dad thinks he's a gourmet chef, but everything he makes is awful. Actually, awful is too kind a word to describe my dad's cooking. Maybe "disgusting beyond belief"?

Luckily, my dad never makes breakfast, because he's usually out painting in his studio in the backyard. He says he loves the early morning light.

Philo, Emily, and I make our way into the kitchen. Sure enough, Dad's at the stove.

"Dad?" Emily asks cautiously. "You're . . . making breakfast?" Even in a situation this upsetting, she doesn't lose her new accent.

"Good morning, honey!" he says cheerfully. "I sure am! Hungry?"

"But, Dad," I say, pointing to the window, "you're missing the beautiful morning light."

He salts whatever disgusting thing is in the pan. "I am. And I still love the light right at sunrise. But for the paintings I'm doing right now, I prefer the light of sunset. So for the next couple of weeks, I can cook you breakfast!"

"Does this mean you won't be able to cook dinner?" Emily asks hopefully.

Dad laughs. "Of course not! Now, who wants turnip turnovers?"

He's holding a big sizzling green blob on the spatula. I'm not a turnip expert, but I'm pretty sure they're not usually green.

Emily and I start talking at the same time, firing off excuses one after the other. "Sorry but . . . Ihavetoeatcerealforaspecial homeworkassignment–I'mallergictoturnips– onaturnipfreediet–fastingforworldpeace– Ialreadyatebreakfast . . . I HAVE TO GET TO THE OFFICE!" I finish loudly just as Emily pauses to take a breath.